WARBLER COTTAGE ROMANCES

The endearing Van Herewaarden family will capture your heart in this compelling romance series set in the Netherlands from the 1930s to the 1960s. Bask in the warm, nurturing love and be inspired by the deep-rooted faith that permeates their home, the Warbler Cottage, and unites them through times of sorrow and joy, tragedy and triumph.

The Complete Saga of the Van Herewaarden Family

The Discerning Heart introduces Marion Verkerk, employed as governess to Baron Reinier Van Herewaarden's daughter, Inge, whose mother is dying of cancer. Marion's faith is severely tested when both Reinier and Jaap Dubois, a bohemian artist, fall in love with her.

A Longing Fulfilled follows sixteen years later. Inge's childhood friend Bram Dubois loves her and wants to marry her. But she fears following the missionary doctor to Suriname. Can her love for God—and for Bram—overcome her fears of the unknown?

A Gleam of Dawn takes place twelve years later and focuses on Inge's half-brother Harro as he pursues the lovely, enigmatic Judith. Although he wins her love, she harbors a painful secret that threatens to destroy their marriage.

By Jos van Manen Pieters:

The Discerning Heart
A Longing Fulfilled
A Gleam of Dawn

Warbler Cottage Romances

A GLEAM OF DAWN

Jos van Manen Pieters

Fleming H. Revell
A Division of Baker Book House
Grand Rapids, Michigan 49516

The Warbler Cottage trilogy was originally published in the Dutch language as *Tuinfluiter Trilogie.* This volume appeared under the name *Als de Tuinfluiter Zwijgt.* Original editions Copyright © 1967 Uitgeversmij J. H. Kok B. V. Kampen, The Netherlands.

Translation into English by J.W. Medendorp.

Library of Congress Cataloging-in-Publication Data

Manen-Pieters, Jos van.
   [Als de tuinfluiter zwijgt. English]
   A gleam of dawn / Jos van Manen Pieters.
     p.   cm.
   Translation of: Als de tuinfluiter zwijgt.
   ISBN 0-8007-5437-9
   I. Title.
PT5881.23.A5A813   1992
839.3'1364—dc20
                                       91-37647
                                           CIP

Published by Fleming H. Revell
a division of Baker Book House Company
P.O. Box 6287, Grand Rapids, MI 49516-6287

ISBN: 0-8007-5437-9

Second printing, February 1993

Printed in the United States of America

Warbler Cottage Romances

A GLEAM OF DAWN

❧ Chapter 1 ❧

Harro Van Herewaarden had not considered the city of Constantine worthy of a single favorable thought until he stood face-to-face with her.

He had noticed her earlier that afternoon, but no one had bothered to introduce them.

The cocktail party was unbearably boring, and the heat of the Algerian afternoon made him yearn for a good Frisian freeze, or at least a dose of Dutch autumn wind. After a time he managed to get involved in a rather boring conversation with an American doctor who asked him everything but appeared indifferent to his answers.

When the good doctor finally realized that he was talking to someone from the Netherlands, he informed Harro that he had a compatriot present among the guests, Miss Judith Uytenbogaard, a singular beauty. He so mutilated the difficult pronunciation of *Uytenbogaard* with his American accent that Harro had to ask him to spell it before he recognized it as a Dutch name.

The doctor scanned the hall and then nodded in the direction of the windows. "The tall brunette over there."

From that moment on, Constantine held a certain intrigue for Harro. He stood leaning against a doorpost for a minute or so, waiting until the girl was finished speaking with the young man who—busily gesticulating—was carrying on a conversation with her in French.

Lovely hodgepodge of nationalities here, he thought critically. *They are all talking to one another, but they are not really interested in one another. Thus the complete lack of atmosphere, no doubt.*

He turned his attention again toward the young lady by the window and was delighted, after many months, to meet someone who spoke his own language and grew up in a similar environment.

The doctor had put his finger on it; this Judith Uytenbogaard was indeed a singular beauty, due in large part to her height. She was at least a head taller than the other women in the group.

Harro, who was six-foot-three, stared with appreciation at the extremely feminine lines of her long figure.

She felt his stare, and her dauntless eyes glanced quickly and defiantly in his direction.

She caught him staring eagerly, and he felt embarrassment warm his cheeks. Nevertheless, he remained standing where he was.

As soon as the young man with whom she was speaking was claimed by another, Harro set out in her direction.

"Miss Uytenbogaard."

"I do not believe I know you," she coolly replied in French. Suddenly it occurred to her that he had addressed her in Dutch and had spoken her name without a trace of an accent.

Harro observed with satisfaction how the expression on

her face softened. Her aversion gave way first to surprise, then to delighted comprehension.

She appreciates this as much as I do, he realized, and the realization allowed him to speak in a more familiar tone. "Nor I you," he answered casually, "but I know the password."

"Which is . . ." She continued in French, but her eyes had begun to twinkle.

"Kale and sausage," Harro replied.

She bridged the remaining distance between them. "You do know how to hit a person's weak spot," she confided. "Do you miss Dutch cooking, too?"

They laughed together and he introduced himself.

"Have you been in Constantine long?" she asked.

He shook his head. "I only come here from time to time. I am working as a consultant on an irrigation project a couple hundred miles to the west."

"In what capacity?"

"As an agricultural engineer. And what do you do?"

"I am a nurse, also acting as a consultant. But they have had me here long enough. In a few weeks I return."

"I am sorry," he gallantly offered. "Why are you returning?"

She looked up at him through her eyelashes. "Maybe I miss kale and sausage," she replied. It was said in jest, but she could not have made it any clearer that her affairs were none of his business. An unmistakable guardedness entered her disposition and expression, which did more to arouse his curiosity than to discourage it.

He considered it worth the effort to get better acquainted with this Judith Uytenbogaard, and even though the allotted time of a few weeks was totally inadequate, it was better than nothing.

He carried on with a neutral conversation and took the opportunity to observe the girl more closely.

She had to be between twenty-five and thirty years old, and the tint of her skin revealed that she must have spent quite some time in a warm climate. She was not gorgeous, per se, but she had a well-formed, determined face that lent her noble disposition an extra accent of spirit.

Her hair was shoulder length and dark. It was full, but fell without much curl along the sides of her face and behind her ears. She was rather curt with her answers, but in her reserve there was no trace of girlish skittishness or awkwardness.

She gave such an impression of maturity that Harro found himself amazed that she was unmarried.

After some time, she announced that she had to return home, and Harro immediately asked whether he, as her compatriot, might not offer her his services as escort.

Her eyebrows rose slightly. "Please, you do not have to leave this exciting party on my account," she noted sarcastically.

He gave an expressive grimace.

"Don't you like these little gatherings?" she asked.

"There are obligations one fulfills with difficulty," he confessed.

In order not to offend the host, however, who might have been her friend, for all he knew, he added by way of mitigation, "They are not all equally boring. If you are fortunate, you can meet interesting people—like today."

Judith took in his compliment with a surreptitious smile, which gave him license to go one step further.

"I would very much like to speak my mother tongue for a while longer," he confided to her. "Couldn't we perhaps find a place where it is a bit cooler and continue with our acquaintance?"

She looked directly into his eager blue eyes, and he seemed young to her, in spite of his respectable size.

"Or have you no more time?" he pressed when she remained silent.

"An hour," was all she said, yielding to his charm.

Not long thereafter they found themselves sitting across from each other at a small rectangular table in a shady, breeze-cooled restaurant.

Judith asked herself with astonishment why she had allowed herself, actually against her will, to be taken in tow by this big child.

Was it only because he was the same nationality? Or had his open admiration released something in her that she had considered effectively suppressed?

She had been a fool to succumb to that weakness; but having taken the first step, she was now obligated to take the second.

In three weeks she would be gone.

What harm could there be in allowing herself to absorb some of this innocent adulation until then, as healing balm on an old wound?

She looked attentively at the young man who sat across from her.

He had blond hair above dark-rimmed glasses, and fine, decided lips in a thin face that was tanned by the sun.

Certainly not without character, but definitely, albeit slightly, younger than herself. Why then such a youthful impression? Or was it only due to the striking slimness of that long body, to which a certain portliness in later years would lend the lacking air of dignity?

She was privately amused by these thoughts that arose in her while they carried on their light conversation.

"Have you done more work outside the country?" Harro asked.

"Yes, I have," she related. "Before I came here, I was in Pakistan and in Persia, and I even worked for a while at a base on the frozen tundra of northern Alaska. Without a doubt the cheapest way to see the world," she added, "at least on the trips to and from. In Alaska things were different, but as far as the rest are concerned, there is little difference between one primitive land and another when it comes to caring for the sick."

"They must have been very difficult years for you," Harro offered. "You must have a great deal of neighborly love at your disposal."

She released a somewhat disparaging laugh.

"Neighborly love, you say? I am afraid I must deprive you of that illusion."

"You are too modest," he replied. "I do not believe you. But I will pretend and ascribe your distant travels to an admirable spirit of adventure. Would you prefer that?"

She gave him a rather strange look.

"You certainly want to force me on a pedestal," she said with a trace of irritation in her voice. "You will certainly be disappointed when I inform you that that which you call neighborly love and spirit of adventure is in reality nothing other than a cowardly flight."

She thought again of the miserable months before her departure to Pakistan.

Jan Willem, the disconcerting verdict of the doctor, the marriage that fell through at the last minute, and the searing sense of humiliation that followed.

Indeed, her departure from Holland had all the makings of a flight.

She did not understand why she had let this confession escape in the presence of a near stranger. It had moved the superficial conversation to an all-too-personal level, and that was something she had not wanted.

Harro noticed her uncertainty, and it struck a completely different chord in him from her fierce self-confidence.

He leaned a little closer to her over the narrow table. His earnest gaze locked onto her own. "Someone has caused you much pain," he confirmed.

She nodded almost imperceptibly. "Is that a valid excuse?" she shot back in self-accusation.

"You do not need an excuse," he said gently. "But I would like to ask you this: Why have you kept on traveling if you are not driven by a spirit of adventure?"

She played mindlessly with the stone on her ring. "Perhaps you learn only through pain and shame that you cannot escape the restlessness within—no matter what you do."

"Maybe you cannot escape, but you can be healed," Harro answered spontaneously. "By becoming happy again, for example."

Had he gone too far?

Her face was closed to him again.

"Who said I was ever happy to begin with?" she asked flippantly, with her old, rather sarcastic tone of voice. "But let's stop all this serious talk and you tell me something about yourself. Was it long ago that you finished your studies in Wageningen?"

"About a year and a half ago. Because my ultimate destiny lay close to home, my parents insisted that I see something of the world first. I took classes in various universities in the United States for about eight months, and after that I made a lengthy visit to my sister and brother-in-law in Suriname. They have been working there at a missionary hospital in the interior for twelve years now."

Judith bent toward him with sudden interest. "You don't mean Doctor Dubois, do you?"

"Yes!" he affirmed with surprise. "Do you know him?"

She shook her head. "When I first started as a young student at the hospital in Utrecht, he had been gone for a year, but his name was still frequently mentioned. He was the idol of a great many nurses. Your sister must have had a lot of competition."

Harro gave an amused grin. "Ten to one Bram never noticed. He is not that type of person. But I will have to write this to my sister!"

"She must be quite a bit older than you," Judith noted, at the same time fishing for his age.

"Nine years," he promptly answered. "She is thirty-six and the oldest. There are six of us, and we vary considerably in age. I have another sister of seventeen."

"I think it would be fun to grow up in such a diverse family," Judith said with remorse. "I was an only child."

"It is also nice," he readily admitted, "that even though several of us have left home, our parents' home remains the central point where we see one another from time to time. I will be happy to be back home. I do believe that I will never feel at home in this country."

"Why did you take this job, then?" she asked candidly.

He shrugged his shoulders somewhat shyly. "I guess you could call it social conscience. When you have had things as good as I have in life, the least you can do is give a little of your knowledge and a year of your life in the service of others who are less fortunate."

"A voluntary sacrifice to appease the gods," she goaded.

Her comment did not sit well with Harro. "I certainly don't share your view," he said coolly. "I don't see religion as some sort of bargain with God."

The blue eyes behind the glasses suddenly lost their youth. Judith understood that she would have to do some damage control if she wanted to restore the lighthearted atmosphere between them.

She made an eloquent gesture of apology with both hands. "Forgive me. It was very unkind of me to say such a thing. Now you must think that I am a heathen."

The smile returned to his eyes. "Until I see evidence to the contrary," he teased.

For a brief moment there was a hint of confusion in her expression at his unexpected answer. Then she stood up.

"I really must go now, Mr. Van Herewaarden," she said, "although I am sorry that I still am not sure of what the destiny that you referred to might be. Have I understood correctly that you were referring to your future work?"

"And what work it will be!" he concurred overconfidently. "But rather than telling you about it, I will let you see it. As soon as we are both back in the Netherlands. Agreed?"

He, too, stood up, and the waiter scurried to their side.

When Harro had settled the bill, he looked at Judith. "What do you think?"

"I can't promise you anything, since I do not have any definite plans for the near future," she said with reserve.

"Oh, I see. You might be traveling to China in six weeks, and from there perhaps to Haiti," he said, aggrieved. "But please don't do it, because you will make it far too complicated for me to find you again. I have the impression that we are far from talked out."

"You may come eat with me Sunday," she proposed to his great surprise. "A good Dutch meal, as far as that is possible. Kale and sausage I cannot guarantee you, I am sorry to say, but I will do my best."

"I am sure it will be delicious—whatever it is," Harro assured her.

Later that evening, as he made the trip down dusty roads back to the settlement two hundred miles away, he had plenty of time to reflect on his remarkable day.

He had driven to Constantine early that morning on business, and was completely unaware at the time that one of the influential persons with whom he had to speak would be giving a cocktail party that afternoon. It was an obligation from which he could not back out, after such a kindly extended invitation, not even with the excuse that he was not, strictly speaking, dressed for the occasion, since his objection was pushed aside by the other as unimportant.

After the promising acquaintance with his attractive compatriot, he lamented little that the day had turned out so differently from what he had anticipated.

"Kale and sausage." He smirked. "How did I ever come up with such an idea?"

He tapped out with his fingers a ditty on the steering wheel of the old delivery truck he had at his disposal, and his mouth turned up in a pleasant smile.

He did not conceal the fact that he was especially looking forward to the coming weekend.

❧ Chapter 2 ❧

Judith Uytenbogaard was boarding with a Swiss doctor's family. Their home stood in one of the newer areas of Constantine and had all the latest modern conveniences. She was for that reason especially pleased with her accommodations.

But she was seldom home. Her work in the traveling medical clinic left her with exasperatingly little free time. When the medical team visited the villages in the outlying areas surrounding Constantine, she had to satisfy herself for nights at a time with a cot.

She had become accustomed in the last few years to living under primitive conditions, and she was able to hold up amazingly well. But then on her days off she doubly enjoyed the inviting luxury of her temporary dwelling.

On this particular Sunday morning she awakened with the vague awareness that there was to be something special. She stretched luxuriously and needed but a few seconds to remember what was on the agenda: Her precise blond compatriot was coming to dinner!

She was thoroughly aware of how she had affected him at their previous encounter, and she was woman enough to derive a secret satisfaction from it. As far as she was concerned, he was a charming lad, to whose visit she sincerely looked forward.

She looked at her watch and with a flurry of activity jumped out of bed to begin her day by indulging in a leisurely bath.

When she was ready, she selected a light white sundress from her wardrobe. She brushed out her hair and put on a touch of makeup.

Into all these ordinary activities a celebrative note had crept, and as she stood before the mirror, looking into her own shining eyes, she asked herself what she was doing. Getting revenge on Jan Willem? Ridiculous. After all, it was not as if no man had ever looked at her in all these years!

She remembered Alaska, where the American soldiers used to be so attentive to her. But they were for the most part married men who were simply looking for an adventure.

This Harro Van Herewaarden was different.

The unmistakable ease with which he moved was no indication of a bored jet-setter, but of an inborn art for living that lacked all pretense.

It would not surprise her, however, if he had never had a girlfriend.

In the meantime he was, in spite of his twenty-seven years and his engineer's title, an overgrown boy, idealistic enough to place a woman on a pedestal, and that attracted her to him.

She hummed as she tried to restore some order to her room and put coffee on. She had already done all the preparations for the meal on Saturday.

It was a beautiful day—clear and warm. Too warm, actually, for working, but perfect for those who had no other task but to relax.

Judith pushed the balcony doors open somewhat further and set up two easy chairs on the now-shaded little balcony. She sat down on one of the chairs, her left arm draped over the back of the chair.

She had spent several Sundays in this same way, pampering herself with a lazy chair and a few delicacies, but all those days lacked what gave this day its special sheen: the companionship of a person with whom to exchange ideas.

She gave herself over to a rather sarcastic self-analysis and reflected that she must have subconsciously been very lonely if it meant so much to her that someone had shown her some attention.

She stood up and looked over the railing of the balcony for a while at the activity in the street below. There were three occupied stories below her, and she did not immediately recognize Harro's old truck when he drove up. But after he had stepped out and his eyes scanned the enormous facade, she caught sight of him and could not refrain from giving a wave of welcome. He noticed her and waved back.

It was only then that the thought ran through her like a shock: Suppose he had not followed up on her request? She laughed at herself. It was, after all, he who had been so keen on getting to know her better.

But as she stood waiting for him by the door of her apartment, the rather bitter conviction arose in her that things were in fact otherwise, and that in spite of the self-conscious disposition she had afforded herself, she had a far greater need for his attention and interest than he did of hers. After all, how did things stand?

This lad had been working for months at an inhospitable outpost in the company of a few men in a strange country in which he did not feel at home. Suddenly he meets a compatriot who by his standards did not look too bad. Was it any surprise that under such circumstances he became infatuated and expressed the wish to meet her again in order to break his monotonous existence? But in a short while he would be returning to the Netherlands and would have whatever he wished there: a home, a large, tight-knit family, work he loved, friends and acquaintances undoubtedly in great quantity. A closed circle of happiness and harmony woven around his life.

And what did she have? If she were to go back now, after an absence of four and a half years, what would she find?

Her former fiancé the husband of another woman, her acquaintances spread here and there, her father dead, her mother remarried during her stay in Algeria to a man who was for her a complete stranger.

Without mercy she totaled the accounts: Judith Uytenbogaard would be out of place in her own land if she were not careful, and she knew it would be advisable not to be too cold to this friendly young man. She might, after all, need him rather desperately when they returned.

This thought definitively determined her disposition toward him.

When they stood facing each other, she greeted him warmly.

"You certainly do not have it too bad here, Miss Uytenbogaard," Harro offered as he wiped his brow. "The only thing you lack is an elevator."

To that she agreed wholeheartedly and added, "Please, call me Judith."

Harro was pleasantly surprised that she had abandoned the reserve that had characterized their last meeting.

They were quickly engaged in an animated conversation.

He sat down in the chair Judith pointed out to him but immediately turned it halfway around so he could observe her as she moved through the room to pour coffee for both of them.

She told him with affection about the Swiss doctor and Mrs. Von Braun with whom she lived, both of them lively in spite of their fifty-plus years and exceptionally kind toward her from the very beginning. They had left early that morning to visit a friend who lived outside the city, but Harro might meet them later.

"It was also their doing that I was invited to the cocktail party this past week," she told him as she came to sit across from him, cup in hand.

"Doctor Von Braun is democratic enough to have no problem introducing a lowly nurse to the upper crust of Constantine."

"Why should he?" Harro asked laconically, not put out in the least.

She laughed her quick, sarcastic laugh. "You do not understand, my good fellow, the gap that exists all over the world between doctors and nurses. Believe me, Doctor Von Braun is a rare bird."

Harro grinned somewhat disbelievingly. "And do you really have such high regard for those appalling cocktail parties?" he asked curiously.

"Of course not," she answered promptly, "but if you are lucky, you can meet some nice people there—like last week."

They laughed together because she had repeated his statement of the week before nearly word for word.

Their common mirth enhanced the relaxed mood between them. Each motivated by the evident affection of the other, they put their best feet forward, and as they teased and joked and explored new ground, the time slipped through their fingers.

While Judith prepared the lunch, Harro looked through a

couple of newspapers lying on the table, but he was always fully aware of her presence.

The white of her sundress was so bright against the tanned skin of her neck. Over and over again it struck him the way in which she held her head when she was busy with something. The gracious confidence of her long, well-formed figure spoke to his imagination.

He could not help but build a decor around her in his thoughts—the decor of the House of Herewaarden, the old family estate where he would reside when he returned home.

In the afternoon it became very warm.

With long, cool glasses next to them, they lazed back in their chairs, and an inevitable lethargy overtook them.

"At this hour there are actually only two things you can do in this heat," Harro offered. "Swim or sleep."

"As far as I am concerned, you may," she teased. "You must look precious when you sleep."

He shook his head. "I would rather watch you."

Her blush was obvious, even under the brown of her skin. "Why?"

"I think that would be nice," he said simply.

Judith felt warm within at how easily he had said it and had meant it, too, but permitted herself nothing that might turn their time together into some banal episode.

"When you return home shortly—how long have you been away from Holland?" Harro asked.

"About four and a half years."

He whistled between his teeth.

"Do you think that is a long time?"

"Terribly long. Although four countries in five years is a pretty heavy schedule, isn't it? Wasn't it difficult to come by all those jobs?"

She shook her head. "There are various organizations for aid to underdeveloped countries. If you have a few contacts and have a good grasp of your trade, then you can be sent out for a year. You just won't get rich from it."

"And Alaska?"

"That was my reaction to the mysterious East. There came a moment when I was so tired of the heat and all that went along with it that I went to the other extreme."

"And now you're right smack dab back in the heat. No regrets?"

"Not today, anyway," she said with a hint of flirtation. She fielded his amused look and lowered her eyes.

Her hand hung down next to her chair, and she was swinging it slowly back and forth. Her hands were long and brown, with clear, polished nails.

Taking the risk that she might find him a pest, Harro again asked a question. He still knew so little about her. "Are your parents still alive, Judith?"

She opened her eyes again. "My father died less than a year after I left home. I was in the middle of a cholera epidemic in Pakistan. We were working practically around the clock, and the news hardly affected me, under the circumstances. He had been long buried before I was finally aware of what I had lost.

"After three years my mother married a friend of my father's. I had never met him, since they had begun their acquaintance after I left, and I did not return from Algeria for the wedding. Perhaps I could have arranged something; perhaps not. But I did not dare. After four years I did not yet dare return there."

In her voice could be detected a vague astonishment at her own attitude, and Harro wondered what could have changed her mind since then.

"And why did you not dare?" he risked, taking advantage of her open mood.

"Oh, I am talking nonsense, of course," she complained. "Why do I talk so much to you? What you must think of me!"

"That you robbed the Bank of the Netherlands as a youth and got at least a half-million," he said flatly.

She was knocked completely off balance. Then she had to laugh. "Silly! You don't mean it."

"No, I don't mean it." Suddenly he became very serious. "There must have been a man back there whom you wished to avoid; the man who hurt you. I would like to get my hands on him."

"You are a sweet boy," she said tenderly, "but it doesn't matter anymore. At some point I woke up again. I have examined my present life and asked myself what is left of the Judith Uytenbogaard of five years ago. At that very moment I realized that no man is worth becoming an eccentric old maid for. I've had enough of living differently from everyone else."

"I did not know the Judith of five years ago," he joked, "but you can take it from me that the Judith of now is worth at least as much as the other one." He gave her an amused grin. "You act as though you just missed the last train out."

"Don't laugh, you pest," she protested. "I'm serious. I am twenty-eight years old, and I'm tired of never having a place to call home. I want to be a common housewife behind a cozy pot of tea, and that's why I am going back to Holland. There is bound to be some widower there, with two sweet children, who needs a wife. You wouldn't perchance know of such a person, would you?"

With the final comment her voice again took on a cynical tone. The remark she was expecting did not come, and finally she had to lower her eyes before the strange look with which her companion seemed to probe her soul.

"Oh, well," she suddenly reflected, "maybe it's nothing. Maybe I would be bored with such a tame existence after three months anyway."

"That would depend entirely on who was sitting on the other side of that teapot," Harro concluded.

❦ Chapter 3 ❧

During the short while remaining to Judith in Constantine they met together several times. Never before had Harro driven the dusty trail between the settlement and the city so often in such a short period of time. All his free time was expended on these visits.

Under normal circumstances such intense pursuit of a new friendship would seem overdone, he reasoned, but seeing that he only had three weeks, he had to take advantage of them to get to know her as well as possible.

The feelings she had evoked in him were so unique, compared to what he had felt for other girls, that he had already cleared out the place of honor for her in his future.

But haste was not part of his nature.

He wanted to be certain that he was not mistaken in his first impression of her, and this drove him to seek out her companionship over and over again.

The atmosphere between them was that of camaraderie.

Occasionally a light flirtation came through, and just as frequently a dissonant chord, when Judith had one of her cynical outbursts. She was surprised by the way Harro courted her, and at times she even doubted whether that was his intention.

He had not so much as made an attempt to touch her. She vacillated between two possibilities: Either he had no intention other than his friendly companionship, or he was in fact mulling over serious plans.

The latter possibility made her a bit wary. This lad should not end up with some woman disillusioned by life's inequities. He needed someone fresh and idealistic, like himself.

Her better self told her that she should not encourage him. After all, what good would she be for him?

She would be better off simply to stick to the plans she had made before she met him and look for a widower with children. There had to be children. That fact alone would relieve her of the baseless but nevertheless stubborn feeling of guilt that had clung to her since her break with Jan Willem, especially when she met men who more or less courted her favor.

Ever since she had met Harro Van Herewaarden, she found herself thinking even more frequently than before of the darkest period of her life.

She had been very proud of her fiancé, Jan Willem Scheppers. He was a bear of a man—broad and tall—future owner of a booming business that had been passed down from father to son for generations. Each and every one of them had been ambitious, and all expanded what had been left to them.

A rich and certain future awaited them both.

When their wedding day was in sight, Jan Willem had insisted that they both undergo a complete physical examination before the wedding.

Judith had been rather puzzled by the request.

"What if they find something wrong with him?" she had said to her mother. "That would not make him any less important to me."

She had never thought about herself. She was strong and lithe and with a zest for life. She went to the doctor without a hint of fear.

For that reason, the blow was so much more devastating.

She was in perfect health, but the doctor detected something unusual and sent her to a well-known gynecologist for further tests. She was tested again, more thoroughly and more painfully.

Her mother had accompanied her this time, and she was there when the doctor pronounced the irrevocable sentence: She would never have children.

Mrs. Uytenbogaard became the spokesperson for her daughter, timidly asking about a possible operation, but the kindly doctor had simply shaken his gray head, doubtful. "A one in a thousand chance, I'm afraid, to correct such an abnormality."

That evening Judith had to inform Jan Willem. While waiting for the appointment with the gynecologist, she had kept him in the dark because of the fear the family doctor had awakened in her.

But now that her quiet, frightened hope had fled, she could not bear it any longer: He had to share her grief.

Longing for his comfort and compassion, she had delivered her sober report.

When she had finished, he remained silent. She observed his face with an ominous feeling. "Why aren't you saying anything?"

"I have to think this over, Judy. This will have serious consequences. You must see that. Even though right now my heart says, 'Where will I begin without Judith?' my mind says

What will become of the Scheppers company without an heir?

Her heart had gone cold within her; even colder than when the doctor had delivered his fatal message.

He had to think it over.

The following day Jan Willem had returned, very timidly. After an entire night of anxiously weighing the facts, he had come to the decision that it would be best if they simply parted as good friends, circumstances being what they were. His father, with whom he had discussed this painful matter, had advised him to do the same.

Although deeply wounded, Judith had shoved her pride to one side and with great difficulty pulled together a proposal. "And if I have them operate on me? There is but one chance in a thousand, the doctor said, but for you . . ." She could say no more.

Jan Willem had shook his head. "The risk is too great, love."

Her eyes had filled with tears, and he tried, with great discomfort, to lift her spirits. "You'll find someone else, Judy, and then you can adopt a couple of kids. Believe me."

"And why can't I do that with you?" she had defied him.

"How could I do that to Father and Grandfather? After me, no more Scheppers in the business. You must understand that, love!"

"Don't call me love!" she had shouted, crying out from anger and disappointment. "You don't even know what love is! If you really loved me, you wouldn't be like this, so rational and heartless!"

That evening signaled the end of her youth.

The man whom she had loved, with whom she had shared the most intimate moments, whom she had trusted as no other, had dropped her like a brick as soon as she posed a threat to his plan.

The weeks that followed were a nightmare for her.

Jan Willem was very generous, in his own way. She could keep everything that they had already acquired for their future home, and if she wanted a short vacation to overcome the shock, he would gladly arrange everything for her.

The Scheppers company would not miss a few hundred dollars, and he did feel very sorry for her. When Judith heard his proposal, she let loose an ugly, bitter word and forbade her parents to allow him to see her again.

As soon as she saw an opportunity, she had resigned from the hospital where she had been working and within two months was on her way to Pakistan, overflowing with bitterness and rebellion.

This had all taken place four and a half years before, and even Jan Willem had become a faded memory, but the scar that she had received from that blow was continually breaking open.

She had been dismissed and cast aside like a barren branch, a useless vessel.

Whenever she met someone who looked at her the way Harro Van Herewaarden sometimes suddenly looked, the thought of her painful past came to the surface again, and she would have to ask herself what he would do if he knew how things stood with her, that as a woman she was not complete, regardless of how the warm blood pulsed through her veins.

She had never made anyone privy to her secret. All these years she had shielded her personal life from curious onlookers, scrupulously avoiding the place where people knew of her humiliation and pain, even though it meant alienating herself from her own mother.

In this way she was slowly able to win back her sense of self-worth, but she was well aware of how vulnerable she still was.

Why did this blond boy have to come into her life now—just as she was to the point of taking a new tack in life—with his carefree laugh and his open face that demanded trust?

And this surprised her the most: She had given him that trust from the very first day, bit by bit.

During her daily rounds in the clinic, as she injected the children or treated the endless eye infections, her thoughts often turned toward Harro as she tried to determine where she stood with him.

She came to the conclusion that it would be best if she put her cards on the table before she left for the Netherlands. Then she could give him the opportunity to silently slip out of her life before she became too attached to him.

Once he mentioned love, it would be too late. She would betray herself again and would feel abandoned when he withdrew. She did not know how to brace herself to go through all this a second time.

When they were together, however, she could not bring herself to speak the words.

She had in the meantime introduced her compatriot to the Von Braun family. They gave Harro a warm welcome, and the doctor's wife told him the first evening that he should feel free to stop in anytime, even after Judith had left.

He had gratefully accepted their offer. Judith had been right: This Swiss couple made a remarkable pair, and one immediately felt comfortable with them.

Shortly before Judith's departure the four of them had spent an evening together that Harro would remember for a long time.

After a few anecdotes from the doctor's colorful career, which he was able to serve up with great taste, they somehow became involved in a deep discussion on one's overall view of life.

The Von Brauns turned out to be convicted Christians who

did not keep their convictions hidden away in the cupboard.

Harro was very interested in how Judith viewed such matters, but he did not want to ask her directly, abiding by the unwritten rule of his parental home that spiritual affairs are better addressed in an unsolicited, unforced manner.

Her unfortunate comment, "Now you must think that I am a heathen," he had calmly set aside at the time.

The way in which she had said it had given him the distinct impression that religion was definitely not a matter of indifference for her, and his impression had been confirmed on his second visit by a number of details.

He was nearly certain that she had been brought up in the same spiritual climate as he had, but precisely how Judith viewed the big questions of life and death, he could only conjecture.

From some of her cynically tainted comments he had suspected that the shocking experience that had brought about such major changes in her life had also left its mark on her spiritual life.

During the revealing conversation of that evening, his suspicion became a certainty.

Poor girl, he found himself thinking when she had sharply disagreed with him on some point. *What have they done to you, that so much unresolved pain remains in your soul?*

It was an impulse which leapt from his heart, but in the meantime he tried to disarm her lack of trust in God and other people and life through careful arguments.

The conversation was carried out primarily between the two of them. The two older participants had become more or less observers, but they followed the exchange of ideas with great interest. They had not undergone their life of experiences without learning something. They both received the impression that their otherwise reserved tenant was now purposely venting her pent-up anger in order to put the boy on the defensive. His opinions must be of great importance to her.

Harro did his best, but even as he heard himself speak, he knew it was no use. Judith would have to be convinced with something other than words.

The conversation had been carried on in German, out of respect for their hosts. Harro noticed how well Judith was able to express herself in that language, almost better than the French he had heard her speak the first time they had met.

He knew that she had studied in a private high school, but afterwards she had turned her back on the academic and gone into nursing. But her excursions into other lands had done her linguistic abilities more good than another year of schooling ever could have.

She gave every impression of being a woman of the world: cultured, elegant, independent, full of spirit and wit.

But behind it all, Harro detected another Judith, a hurt, lonely young woman who hungered for security and love.

Sometimes this other Judith seemed very near the surface—but then an invisible curtain would fall between them and he would begin to think he was mistaken.

It was well into the night when Dr. Von Braun put an end to the heated discussions and focused his attention on the fact that Harro still had hours of driving ahead of him.

His wife quickly made them all something to eat, and then they took their leave of one another.

At Harro's request, Judith accompanied him to the car.

It was a balmy night with a strikingly beautiful sky.

Once they stood outside in the immense silence, their discussions about God suddenly seemed silly and presumptuous.

Judith felt a desire to put this into words, but instead she said, subdued, "You won't be able to get much sleep tonight."

He looked at his watch.

"It is hardly worth the trouble of going to bed. I'll take a nice cold shower when I arrive, and then go directly to work."

"And just about then you will be very sorry that it got so late."

"On the contrary. It was a very educational evening for me."

She reflected on her aggressiveness and suddenly feared that she had lost him before anything had ever existed between them.

"An educational evening," she repeated bitterly. "No doubt because you discovered how argumentative I am. Wouldn't it be better if we just said good-bye forever, Harro?"

He looked at her with that unique, probing look of his, so young and wide-eyed, and yet so wise.

A breathless silence fell between them, in which she awaited the dismissal she had requested. But his continuing silent examination confused her.

Then he said something amazing, "How I would like to kiss the furrows from your soul, my friend!"

He had caught her completely by surprise, and her mouth began to tremble. "You must not be so kind," she complained. "That is not good for me. That is not at all good for me."

"Let me disagree with you," he said softly. He drew her to himself and caressed her lips with his own, tenderly, without haste.

It was as exciting as it was comforting, and Judith felt completely taken by surprise. Then she regained her presence of mind. She made her way free and said sarcastically, "That was my mouth, Harro, not my soul."

He did not allow himself to be flustered. "Your soul is still so far from mine," he said quietly. "But I will find the way. You just wait."

❦ Chapter 4 ❧

Judith departed twenty-four hours earlier than she had
originally planned. When Harro came to Constantine two
days after their last encounter to wish her a safe journey, she
was not to be found.

Mrs. Von Braun met him at the entrance and invited him
in. The doctor was away. "Judith is not here," she said matter-
of-factly after she greeted him.

"I assume that she will not be gone long," he responded
casually. "She knew I would be coming by this evening to bid
her farewell."

Mrs. Von Braun looked up at his cheerful face; she had
some explaining to do. "It was not very kind of her to let you
come for nothing," she resumed, "but she left today for Al-
giers to visit a couple of friends there before she continued
her journey to Marseilles."

Harro pursed his lips; his expression grew dark. Did this
mean that she did not want anything more to do with him?

"Ma'am," he said curtly, "do you have any idea why Judith is avoiding me? I had the impression that we had become good friends over the last few weeks."

She in return asked him a candid question. "Mr. Van Herewaarden, what were your intentions toward Judith?"

"My intentions? I only wanted to make her happy, nothing more."

"I am happy to hear you say that."

He frowned. "While she has taken the first opportunity to get away from me?"

The doctor's wife stood debating with herself for a moment.

"Please sit down," she said. "I will be honest with you. Judith spoke with me about you before she left. It was certainly not her idea that I would pass that conversation on to you, but maybe it is for the best. She did not avoid you because she could not bear to see you. On the contrary, she cares a great deal for you."

"But why, then?" he asked.

"Judith has no contacts back home anymore after such a lengthy absence," she explained. "She saw that clearly, and when she met you and realized that you, too, would be going back soon, she saw the possibility of gaining a foothold again through you, of developing a new circle of acquaintances. In short, she wanted to put down roots again in the Netherlands. You could be useful for her in the future, and that is why she allowed you to enter her private life. She hardly ever let that happen. She was not liberal with her friendship."

"Well, well," he said sarcastically, insulted by the practical motives that apparently were driving Judith. "I am honored. And then?"

"You must not be angry because she wanted to use you to achieve her goal," Mrs. Von Braun gently admonished him. "People use each other all the time to get ahead. But when our hearts get involved, that is something different. And that is also the reason she left today."

"I still don't get it."

" 'It has gotten out of hand,' she said to me. 'He is too young and too naive. I would only stand in the way of his happiness, and I don't want that. I must leave here before I begin to love him too much, Mrs. Von Braun.' "

"She said that?"

"Word for word."

"But I don't see at all how she could stand in the way of my happiness. I'll be hanged if I see that," he insisted stubbornly.

"Maybe she felt she was too old for you."

"Ridiculous. She is all of one whole year older than I am. We can hardly speak of an age difference here."

The doctor's wife grinned slightly. "In years, maybe," she said, "but a person can be young in years and old in experience."

He stuck his chin out. "It does not make the slightest difference to me what has happened in her life before me," he said loftily.

Mrs. Von Braun rummaged through a drawer.

"Tell her that," she said, her back turned toward him. "Tell her that as soon as you are back in the Netherlands. That seems to be the only way. I know as little as you do about why she does not think she is in a position to make you happy. If she has a secret, she hides it exceptionally well. But there are plenty of obstacles to overcome. I wish you much success."

She gave him a small piece of paper, and he automatically read what was written on it.

"Whose address is this?"

"It is her mother's. She has been married a second time, and that is why she has a different name. At least now you have a contact. Maybe in time Judith will send us her new

36

address, but then again maybe not. She is a wonderful girl, Mr. Van Herewaarden, but also difficult."

He smiled self-assuredly. "I have no doubts about your insight," he said calmly, "but I am still not going to give her up."

Harro had to stay another two and a half months in Algeria; eleven long weeks before his contract expired and someone else came to take his place at the irrigation project.

Not one of those weeks went by without a visit to the doctor in Constantine.

At their home he met the nurse who took Judith's place, a friendly blond girl from Scotland whom he took out once in order to show her around her strange environment. She could not, however, make him forget about her predecessor.

He preferred to find Mrs. Von Braun at home alone and then would try to get her to talk about Judith. They had not heard anything from Judith since her departure. She seemed to think it necessary to vanish from their lives.

At first Harro considered writing her, but he quickly retreated from that idea. She might take steps to make herself unreachable. It was better to exercise a little patience and take the fortress by surprise at the right moment.

Finally he arrived at the point where he would climb the countless steps for the last time to say farewell to the kindly Swiss couple. They were losing a welcome house guest, and said so plainly.

"Harro," Dr. Von Braun had said—they had long since abandoned all formalities—"Harro, next year about this time we will also be home. We are counting on you to come to Switzerland to be our guest for a few weeks."

He accepted the invitation heartily. "Maybe I will bring Judith along with me," he suggested overconfidently.

The doctor lowered his head and laughed heartily.

But his wife seriously followed up on his comment. "Are you still planning to look her up?"

Harro nodded. "Not only that. I'm planning a lot more."

"May we come to the wedding?" the doctor teased.

"As far as I am concerned, the sooner the better!"

The three of them laughed together as at a good joke, but as soon as Harro had left, Mrs. Von Braun said to her husband, "Let's hope he succeeds in winning her over. Judith has undoubtedly had some bitter experiences in her life, and he is just the right person to restore her faith in humanity. We must continue to think about them, Karl."

Think she said, but she meant pray, and he knew it. She shunned big words and pious theories, as did he. Their Christian life was 99 percent practice.

The following morning Harro began his journey home. After a stopover of a couple of days in Rome, where his sister Charlotte was working as a fashion designer at one of the well-known fashion houses, he continued his journey toward the Netherlands, completing this last leg by plane.

When he arrived at Schipol International, the entire welcoming committee was present: two cars full of family members who had quibbled for days about who would pick him up, until the *pater familias* finally decided they should all go. That was an immediate baptism by fire for Harro, lest he had forgotten what it was like to have a large, teasing family to put up with.

His parents came in their own car with his father's younger brother, Diederick, who was handicapped, and his wife, Juliette, whom he had married later in life. This uncle had played a major role in Harro's life, and he was greatly honored that he and Aunt Juliette were among the party.

The other car, belonging to his older brother, Rein, carried five people to the airport: Rein and his young wife, Paula, their small heir of two years, the youngest two of the Van

Herewaarden family, Erik, a student at the Economic Technical School in Leiden, and Lucy, seventeen, who was still in high school and as a result of this escapade hopelessly behind in her homework.

The ten of them stood in a bunch, and their cheerful shouts were plenteous.

"What did I tell you, Mother?" Erik cried. "He has gotten even taller in that year! You better have an addition put on his bed!"

Harro, laughing, bent over his mother to give her a kiss.

"You just let Erik talk," he consoled her. "It just seems that I am taller because I am so thin from the heat and strange food."

He looked around him with great satisfaction at all the familiar faces.

He caught hold of little Reinier, who found the shoulders of this uncle frightfully high and made no bones about it.

Paula comforted her frightened son with candy while Harro was bombarded with questions about his trip and Charlotte, whom he had seen earlier that day.

"Let's go get a cup of coffee," he proposed. "Then I will tell you everything you want to know."

While the group looked for a table in front of one of the large windows, he slipped away for a moment to the telephone.

He had decided on the airplane to call Judith's mother as soon as possible to find out about her whereabouts, and he could do that better here than at home, where his teasing teenage brother and sister were always underfoot, not to mention his lovely mother with her woman's intuition and natural curiosity.

His conversation lasted no longer than three minutes, but just before he rejoined the group, he was missed.

"Where is Harro?" his mother asked, looking around the group.

"He is standing over there talking to someone on the telephone," Lucy pointed out.

Harro was just approaching, and heard what she had said. He encircled her slender neck with his sinewy hands. "Spy!" he laughingly scolded.

She wriggled loose and looked up at him. "Harro had to call his girlfriend," she teased. "Tell the truth, Harro. Did you have to call your girlfriend?"

He tugged at her blond ponytail. "No, smart aleck," he retorted, "my mother-in-law."

It worked exactly as he had expected it would. Everyone laughed at his words, but no one attached any importance to them.

And so it had to stay for the time being.

⚜ Chapter 5 ⚜

J udith's mother, who for almost a year had the name *Mrs. Van Alkemade*, lived in Wassenaar. The telephone conversation that Harro had with her was brief, but it gave him exactly what he had been looking for.

He had introduced himself as an acquaintance of her daughter's from Algeria, who wanted to convey the greetings of the Von Braun family, with whom she had lived in Constantine.

Mrs. Van Alkemade told him without hesitation what he wanted to know: Shortly after her return home, Judith had accepted a private nursing job at the home of a wealthy old woman in Nijmegen who had needed nursing help as the result of a stroke.

The condition of her patient did not leave her with much free time. She came home very irregularly, but if he wanted to jot down the address, she was more than willing to look it up for him.

He had given her his heartfelt thanks for her willingness and soon knew the number and street by heart.

While they were on their way home, he pondered when he would be able to go to Nijmegen to look her up.

If Judith thought he would simply give up after her hasty departure from Constantine, she had greatly misjudged him. For the umpteenth time he asked himself what all her reserve was about. Why didn't she want to give her affection for him the chance to grow into something deeper that could give her life a new shine?

So deeply was he embroiled in this thought that his father had to ask him the same question twice before he returned to reality.

He apologized for his absence of mind and again gave his parents a detailed report about their second daughter, who was busy in Rome building a career that was clicking along like a clock.

He described for them the apartment in which Charlotte lived and the coworkers from the fashion house to whom she had introduced him.

"She feels at home in that little world, like a fish in the water," he summed up, "and I had the impression that she is very popular among her colleagues. In any case, you don't have to be concerned about her. She is very able to look after herself."

"I would rather she look for a good husband," her father complained.

His wife simply laughed at him. "You better not let Charlotte hear you say that! That child has worked her whole life for this, and now that she has conquered this position, she will not quickly leave it for the sake of a man. Besides, she feels that twenty-five is far too young to be tied down."

"Just be happy, Reinier, that Marion thought differently about these things back then," Diederick interjected into the conversation.

"Marion?" Harro's father teased. "By the time she was twenty-three, she had already achieved her life's ambition!"

She laid her hand on the arm of her husband, and her eyes laughed into his.

And what an achievement it was, she said to herself.

"There was more romance in the older generation than there is in the younger," Harro opined. "Charlotte could learn a lot from you, Mother. In Moerdijk I'll switch cars, then I can see how Rein and Paula manage it."

"That's right, it's high time that you studied this material, too," his aunt Juliette teased. She continued a while longer on this subject, and Harro was happy to oblige her with light-hearted replies.

But between barbs his attention was focused on his mother.

He leaned to one side behind her and attentively observed her profile. Was it his imagination, or did she appear more fragile and less robust than before he left?

Once he had switched to the other car, he openly asked his brothers and sister, "Is there something the matter with Mother? She seems tired to me."

Rein, surprised by this abrupt comment from his brother, said reassuringly, "A little anemic. Father is concerned about it, but she doesn't pay much attention. She is resting more than before, but she is still just as cheerful, isn't she, Paula? If you could see how well she handles the baby and little Reinier!"

Harro looked at his sister. "You're the only one still at home, Lucy. What do you think?"

"That she would think you were all crazy," she said rather stiffly.

Harro resolved to feel his sister out on this comment when the right moment presented itself.

In the meantime they had arrived in Dintelborg, where Rein and Paula lived in a modern little house and where their father's large leather goods factory was located.

A few years before, Rein had assumed the position of co-director, and Erik, too, would be taken into the business eventually.

Harro himself had never had aspirations in that direction.

He longed to ride on to Borg and see the House of Here-waarden once again. For hundreds of years, it had been the residence of his family. Now only Uncle Diederick and Aunt Juliette led their secluded life there, but he hoped to settle down there himself and blow new life into the proud old estate and everything associated with it.

His father did not love the castle, as the building with the two pointed towers was popularly known.

In his youth, under the rule of his mother, the baroness, for whom nobility and traditions were sacred matters, he learned to regard the place as a cage, and the way of life that accompanied it as a straitjacket that kept him from an uninhibited life-style.

Shortly after he came of age, he went his own way. He invested his money into a bankrupt factory that had grown quickly under his guidance over the years, and he had preferred life in a simple villa to the protocol of the castle.

His first house, the Warbler, was close to the factory in Dintelborg. He had lived there only a few years with his first wife, Magda, and their little daughter, Inge.

Shortly before Magda died from the terrible cancer that ate away at her, he became acquainted with Marion, and with her acquaintance a major change occurred in his life.

He had been a widower less than a year when he was able to win her love, and shortly after the period of mourning, he married her.

His second marriage, unlike the first, which was over before it had even begun, had brought him everything he had ever wanted.

Together they had another five children, and the second Warbler, which they had built in Borg, had been a haven of happiness for them for thirty years.

The villa stood only a fifteen-minute walk from the House

of Herewaarden, where Diederick, after the death of the baroness, lived practically as a hermit, severely handicapped by his physical condition until he, at the age of thirty-three, found a compatible woman.

Harro had spent half his youth at the castle.

At a very young age he had been enchanted by the secrets it held: the antiques, the yellowed family archives, the portrait gallery, all the reminders of the rich, moving past of the lineage into which he had been born. Uncle Diederick had always been a willing guide in this adventure.

The young boy had filled a considerable portion of the lame man's existence. The kinship between them was unmistakable, and Diederick had always regarded Harro as his own child, the son he would in actuality never have.

In the meantime the years marched by.

The rather extensive holdings, of which the castle formed the central point, had for years no longer been self-sustaining. The farms had grown older and the lands, orchards, and forests would have profited much from modern methods of farming and foresting.

It was the profit generated by the leather factory that had kept the family holdings free from tax liens.

For many years an estate manager had been employed to look after the financial matters of the House of Herewaarden. He did so with great discretion, but with the exception of a few minor details, things remained as they had always been.

Diederick, a typical parlor scholar, rarely considered the fact that status quo meant financial loss, and Reinier Van Herewaarden had never been able to muster enough interest in his inheritance to undertake the reorganization of the properties in addition to the direction of his growing, demanding business.

Harro, by way of contrast, had for years delighted in that task. He was brimming with plans and was well prepared to

45

implement them in a professional way because of his studies.

But he still had to suppress his yearning to see the House of Herewaarden for a little while.

Both cars drove directly to the Warbler, although Rein and Paula's made an immediate about-face. They had hired a baby-sitter to take care of the baby, who was just three months old, and Paula thought they had been away from home long enough.

Diederick and Juliette accompanied them inside for a quick cup of tea.

Lucy began the preparations right away. She had become much more independent while Harro had been away from home.

She had literally pushed her mother to an easy chair, ignoring her protests. "You just make yourself comfortable and enjoy the fact that Harro is home again," she smoothly arranged. "Father, you see to it that she does what I say. Erik, you are the only one who may help. Let's go, front and center!"

They playfully made their way toward the kitchen.

"Ever since Erik started coming home on weekends, those two have managed to get along capitally," Marion gratefully observed. "They used to quarrel from the very moment they opened their eyes in the morning!"

Harro knew exactly what she was talking about. He himself had played arbiter on more than one occasion, first between Rein and Charlotte, who were always at each other, and then for these two afterthoughts. In one way or another, he had always managed to stand above the disputing parties, even when he was just a boy.

Now that he had been able to stand at something of a distance, he understood that he must have been an odd, dreamy child with his enormous power of imagination and his interests that were so totally differently directed from those of his turbulent brothers and sisters. It was good that over the years life itself had given him a good handle on reality.

He thought about Judith and stole a grin.

More than anything, she needed a man of flesh and blood, not a dreamer.

When his uncle and aunt made motions to leave after an hour or so, Harro demanded the right to drive them home. He accustomed himself to his father's roomy car after the ancient relic he had at his disposal in Algeria.

After Diederick and Juliette had retreated into their haunt in the west wing of the old house, Harro did not depart immediately.

Ambling nonchalantly, he took in the entire surroundings of the castle, looking over everything and consciously enjoying the beautiful fall colors of the old trees and the lawns, now carpeted with leaves.

The yearning to begin working grew stronger in him as he continued his walk of reacquaintance.

Only as evening fell did Diederick notice his nephew step back into his car and depart by the entrance road. Harro raised a cheerful hand when he spied his uncle behind one of the large windows.

Diederick waited until the car was out of sight, then limped back to his chair, at peace, even though he felt that he was about to have another bout of the bronchitis that marred his life at regular intervals.

He knew he was tired and ill, in no condition to do battle with the problems of the dynamic times in which he lived and incapable of keeping up with its tempo.

He was well aware of all that, but it no longer upset him.

The boy was back, and he would again restore to the House of Herewaarden its *raison d'être*.

✍§ Chapter 6 ɜ❧

The following morning, three of them sat eating breakfast: Reinier, Harro and Lucy. Erik had departed for Rotterdam the previous evening, and Marion was still sleeping.

Between two slices of bread, Harro asked in passing, "Father, how is the Rolls-Royce?" He was referring to the car used by the gardener-chauffeur of the House of Herewaarden to do shopping and run various other errands, which owed its apt nickname to its outdated rectangular shape.

Diederick owned no car for his own use for the very simple reason that he never went anywhere.

Reinier Van Herewaarden grinned. "The Rolls-Royce? It is still plugging along. Why?"

"Then I can use it this week? I have a few things to do and need to go to the city, and tomorrow I wanted to go to Nijmegen to look up an old friend."

His father wrinkled his eyebrows. "You can't show up at a girl's house with that old brick," he said evenly.

Lucy giggled behind her hand.

But Harro was well able to hold up under teasing. "You should have seen what I rode around with in Constantine," he rallied. "Besides, who says it's a girl?"

"No one. But it's obvious. You may take the Chevy."

"What will you use, then?"

"I will take the day off and keep your mother company."

Harro grabbed another slice of bread from the platter. "Just like that?" he teased with the same even tone. "After you have been telling us all these years that work comes before girls?"

"When you are not so young anymore," Reinier said, suddenly serious, "then you make the most of the hours you can spend together. Then work takes a distant second to your girl, Son."

Harro thought he heard a vague sense of despair in his father's words. Old! That was a laugh! At sixty-one, his father was one of the liveliest people he knew, and his mother was only fifty-three. That is not the age at which people normally begin to count their hours together as precious moments. Not even in a marriage that was as happy as that of his parents.

He could come to only one conclusion: His mother was being threatened by some danger that everyone was bravely trying to play down. But he would soon get to the bottom of it, since he was sure his father was at least as worried as Lucy.

The following afternoon he drove to Nijmegen.

The address that Mrs. Van Alkemade had given him appeared to be an old manor from near the end of the last century. It was stately, but without character.

When he rang the doorbell, the door was opened by a young woman whose age was difficult to tell and whom he presumed to be the housekeeper.

He asked if he could speak to Miss Uytenbogaard for a moment. The woman looked at him somewhat absently.

"Oh, the nurse!" she suddenly understood. She asked him to wait in the hall and climbed a broad oak staircase.

Harro stood standing in the middle of the room, which was overloaded with Delft and expensive new furniture. He killed the time by imagining what would have to be disposed of in order to make it a livable room again, and especially what would have to be added to the interior: books and flowers, a few toys, and especially a woman who would give all these things a soul.

After about ten minutes, Judith entered. She seemed strange and unapproachable in her uniform with the impeccable white apron.

He turned when he heard her come in, and searched for her eyes.

She pushed the door shut behind her and leaned against it. Her face was so closed that he had the strong impression that she was going to say, "Excuse me. I do not believe I know you," as she had at their first encounter during that memorable cocktail party in Constantine.

"How did you find me?" she finally asked, almost angrily.

"That doesn't matter," Harro said. "Let's just say that you didn't cover your tracks well enough." He took a couple of steps in her direction and reached out his hand. "Hello, Judith."

Ever so slowly, as though against her will, she placed her hand in his, but she did not return his greeting. "Why did you do this?" she struggled to say.

"Because I fell in love with you back there," he said simply.

For a brief moment her mouth twitched nervously. Then she said stiffly, "But you must have understood that I did not leave without saying good-bye for no reason at all."

"Of course. But don't you think you have been running away from your own feelings long enough? It is high time that you really came home, Judith." He made a vague gesture around him. "Because all this means nothing to you."

"No," she conceded with a flutter of humor. "At least we agree on that much."

Harro still held her hand firmly. "Can you take some time off this evening?" he asked. He could read the struggle within her on her face. "Don't run away, Judith," he curtly cautioned.

"What do you want from me?"

"For the time being I just want to talk to you somewhere where it is quiet. Not here."

"Come pick me up at about eight-thirty," she said, shrugging her shoulders. "Although I must say that I don't see the point."

"Sometimes it is healthy to do things even when you don't see the point," he volleyed. "I won't keep you from your work any longer. Until this evening, Judith."

He went somewhere to eat and whiled away the time by reading all the available magazines and newspapers in the restaurant.

It seemed an eternity before eight-thirty rolled around.

In the meantime, Judith carried on a running dispute with herself. She mechanically reacted to the laboriously uttered words of her patient, whose speech had been affected by the stroke; she automatically carried out her daily activities.

He came and found you, Judith. Think about it. Immediately after his return home, he found you. He is sincere; why are you pushing him away?

But then all those weeks you tried to put him out of your thoughts will be time lost. There can never be anything between you. He is no match for you.

Why not? If you want to get married, why not with him? After all, you gave up the illusion of marrying out of love a long time ago. At least this boy has a lot of attractive qualities.

You shouldn't deceive him. If you tell him the truth and he still wants you, then you will never again have to be ashamed. Then you will be desired for what you are. It is worth the risk.

But I don't dare tell him. Why should he react any differently from Jan Willem, who was so much more obligated to me? I would not be able to bear that kind of humiliation again.

You know very well that he is different from Jan Willem. He would rather spend the rest of his life acting out a charade than treat you so rudely.

But I don't want to get married out of pity or because of some noble gesture. I want to be an equal partner!

The two voices went back and forth and tried to override each other. Judith was exhausted by it all.

When she had completed her duties at eight and dressed in a red suit that she knew particularly flattered her, she still had no idea what she would say to Harro when he came.

He was right on time. While he held the door of the car open for her, he laid his hand briefly on her sleeve. "Are you nervous?"

She nodded.

"Don't be embarrassed," he said, putting her at ease with the smile she so well remembered. "I am, too."

"You wouldn't say that, otherwise," she said rather acridly, defending herself against the charm he exuded. "You were mighty sure of yourself this afternoon."

"A question of self-control," he demurred. "Appearances are deceiving."

A few moments later he remarked, "I know a restaurant just outside the city where we can sit comfortably and quietly. What do you say we get something there?"

"Sure. Why not?" she weakly agreed.

On the way they were both quiet. Only once did Judith open her mouth. "You have a nice car," she said.

"I borrowed it," Harro cheerfully admitted. "But I agree that it is a nice car."

Once they had parked, Harro did not get out immediately. He turned to Judith and said seriously, "Before we go in, there is one thing I want to make clear. It is not my intention to force your feelings. I never expected you to fall into my arms. I only want to resume our acquaintance where it was broken off. Walking off as you did was a silly move. I won't let it end like that. If you have something against me, then you can tell me to my face. Agreed?"

"That was not the reason," Judith softly defended herself. "What would I have against you?"

"Precisely," he resumed without relenting. "I have been breaking my head over that question for the last three months."

Without intending to, he had unleashed an argument. Judith began to berate him passionately. "I have nothing against you, but I wonder what on earth you want with me. I am not young and not pretty and not sweet—and for you, all possibilities are still open. There are enough eighteen-year-old girls in the world who are prepared to eat out of your hand!"

"Thanks," he said dryly. "I am not interested in spindly-legged teenagers. When I choose a woman, she must look like a woman. And what is pretty and sweet I can decide for myself."

His firm words did her good, in spite of it all. "But you . . ." she began.

"But what?"

She could see his sharp profile with the curly blond hair above it. The thought that he could also have curly blond-haired children and would be a model father pierced her heart. She felt a strange, sad sympathy for him, because step by step he was depriving himself of the chance to have such a family—and he did not know it.

"What were you going to say?" Harro again pressed.

"What was I going to say? That you are too good to settle for someone who has been discarded by another!" she threw out passionately.

For a brief moment she perceived an intense anger rise in his eyes. Then he regained his balance. "Will you do me a favor and never say such a thing again?" he asked forcefully. "What you are doing is nursing an old wound, and that is unhealthy. Judith, you cannot do this. Whatever you may have gone through, it was five years ago. You have to close the book on it and be willing to start over again."

She looked at him in silence while her heart ached. *Will I get a new body then, without that little detail that makes it impossible for me to bring your children into the world?* she thought defiantly.

But the words stuck in her throat. She could not bring herself to say it. "My dream is dead," she whispered almost imperceptibly.

Harro took her hands. "God has more than one dream in store for you, my friend. But you have to be willing to accept it. Come on."

He reached over to open her door for her, and thus put an abrupt end to this unexpected personal conversation.

With the autumn wind in their hair, they walked in silence toward the entrance of the restaurant.

❦ Chapter 7 ❧

Harro was not aware of it, but he was a born host. He saw the chance to sweep away the tension between them with a simple gesture and a few selected words, and Judith did not understand how it was possible that she was soon able to carry on a normal, pleasant conversation with him.

They sat in a quiet, sparsely populated part of the restaurant, and before Judith had the chance to be embarrassed at the fact that she had divulged more than was her intention, Harro had taken the lead again.

He crossed his arms on the table and, leaning toward her with interest, insisted, "And now you must tell me everything about your experiences over the last couple of months. How did you happen to end up working here in Nijmegen, in that awful tasteless house?"

"I do have to earn a living, you know," she said soberly. "I was never able to save anything living abroad. I'll grant you that it is not the ideal environment with that suspicious old witch, but the pay is good and I actually view it as a transition period, in which I can quietly reflect on the next stage of my life."

Harro frowned. "Old witch? You mean your patient? Is she unkind to you?"

"She harbors the idea that everyone is out to get her money. She fired three nurses before me. Those who are friendly to her are looking for a place in her will, and those who are unfriendly are making plans to steal from her. Just between you and me, I got the details on my predecessors from the housekeeper, whom she also suspects."

"And to which category do you belong?"

Judith made an innocent gesture. "To the first, although I must admit I show her nothing more than professional courtesy. You know, when it comes right down to it, for all her money, she is a pitiful wretch. She does not have long to live, and she knows it, but she still fills all her time with mistrust and suspicion."

The coffee Harro ordered was served, eliminating the old woman from their conversation.

Harro looked attentively at the woman who sat across from him. Her brown skin had faded somewhat after three months of being indoors, but the red outfit she was wearing seemed to share something of its glow with her cheeks. Her hair had a more contemporary cut than in Algeria, and her eyes were larger and more expressive than he had remembered.

He wanted to take that warm, lively face between his hands; he wanted to prevent all the ghosts from her past from coming between them anymore. But for the time being he did nothing other than nod disarmingly toward her. "You look stunning," he said after the waiter had retreated. "That red puts out so much warmth that you could melt a glacier."

She nodded in agreement. "Colors are important. I feel so

much more like a woman in this outfit than I do in that cold, impersonal uniform."

"Then if I ever get sick," Harro joked, "you can take care of me in red. I guarantee you, I'll be better in a day."

"In that case, sir, it would not be worth the while to take the job," she primly returned.

"Oh, but I'll fake it," he promptly promised. "Weeks at a time, if I have to. You won't be sorry, nurse."

The recovery of their former lightheartedness was good for the tension between them. With a sense of relief they drank their coffee.

Then Harro asked, "What is your stepfather like, Judith? Have you been able to hit it off with him?"

"He's a good man, I think. He is certainly good for Mother, if you can believe her."

A cynical tone entered her voice as she continued, "I stayed with them for two weeks, but long before they were over, I had the impression that he was paying more attention to me than he was to Mother."

What a surprise, Harro thought in a brief moment of strict objectivity. *I wouldn't mind having such a stepdaughter at home.*

"That was one of the reasons I went back to work so quickly," Judith explained. "Not because I did not feel up to the situation, but I found it sad for Mother."

"Is that why you spend so little time at home?" Harro asked, putting aside all objectivity.

That dirty old man, he thought vengefully.

"Not just for that reason," Judith answered. "I have really grown apart from my mother these last few years; we don't have much to say to each other anymore."

She interrupted herself. "How did you know that I spend so little time at home?"

Suddenly the old reserve and guardedness entered her expression again. He should not have gone talking behind her back with her mother. If he ever came to know anything about her secret, she would be the one to determine when and in what way it would happen.

Harro decided to lay his cards on the table. "I called your mother. Mrs. Von Braun gave me her address. That is how I found you here. Are you still angry that I came?"

She hesitated with her answer. It was as though she needed every bit of energy to withstand his penetrating look.

Slowly her sense of proportion returned. She knew that her fear was unfounded. Her mother would never discuss such intimate things with a stranger out of nowhere, especially not by telephone.

"No," she said finally, "angry is not the right word. You simply put me on the spot. You are more persistent than you appear, Harro Van Herewaarden. I am afraid that I underestimated you."

He laughed heartily, exposing his white teeth, and Judith sensed that her reserve had not withstood his overwhelming manner. Her tense mouth relaxed, and against her will she laughed with him.

"Who knows what other surprises might still await you?" Harro suggested.

It all seemed so strange to Judith. That evening in Constantine she thought she had solved the problem he posed by disappearing without a trace from his life. But she had not succeeded.

Even if she were to tell him outright that she did not want anything to do with him anymore, he would continue to surround her with his attention until she had been softened up and her longing for the protection of a solid marriage overcame her objections.

But did she really want him to go?

Hadn't his sudden appearance that afternoon shown her

how endlessly colorless the string of days had been without him here in the Netherlands?

His optimistic, uncomplicated view of life courted her more than she wanted to admit.

At a quarter after ten she was sincerely sorry that she had to signal her departure. She still had to help her patient before going to bed and therefore could not set her own time of return.

On their return trip to the city, their conversation centered again around the sick old woman who saw gold diggers all around her.

Harro, picking up on a crazy idea, earnestly advised Judith, "If she gets on you again about her money and will, you just tell her that you don't have the slightest interest, since you will soon be asked to marry a young nobleman and will go to live with him in a castle and will have everything that your heart desires."

Judith laughed as though it were a good joke. "Sure, that is the least I can do to impress her," she mocked.

It was amusing to Harro that she had no idea how much truth there was hidden in his words. He had told her a great deal about his family, but nothing about his background. As far as that was concerned, he was like his father, who had buried his title as much as possible and given his children a democratic upbringing in every respect.

But when he introduced Judith to his family in Borg, as was his intention, he would eventually have to tell her about his situation there. He hoped that he would be able to communicate to her his love for the House of Herewaarden. One of his favorite fantasies was to wander with her over the lands of the castle and let her see the world of which his life consisted.

As the Chevrolet turned down the tree-canopied street

where she worked, he asked, "When can we do this again? Next week?"

Judith had dismissed her inner resistance. "I would like that," she said gently.

They made a date and the moment came for them to say good-bye. Harro turned off the engine but remained behind the steering wheel.

"I have to go now," Judith said.

Her face was but a pale spot in the darkness.

"Yes," Harro agreed, "I know. I was just wondering whether I should give you a kiss before you go."

Her puzzlement at his comment was tangible, but he continued, "Last time I did not enjoy it."

"Is that so?" she asked.

"I am afraid," he went on, "that you will disappear again, and I really don't want to have to pay for every kiss with twelve weeks of loneliness."

She remembered the sweet excitement she had experienced with his first and only kiss under the wide, star-sprinkled sky of Africa.

A shiver ran through her. "I promise that I will not run away this time," she said modestly.

He kissed very differently from other men she had known. Not brutally and forcefully, as an inevitable prerequisite to other things, but as though kissing were itself a high art, worthy to be practiced with dedication and refinement for its own sake.

When he released her, she leaned against his shoulder. "I am unable to resist you," she confessed.

He laughed in the dark. "Why must you?" he asked.

❧ Chapter 8 ❧

Harro had been home for a week, but he could still not get used to the fact that his mother did not appear at the breakfast table in the morning. The others appeared not to notice, since no one ever alluded to it.

Toos Brinkman, his mother's devoted help, brought a heaping plate upstairs during the morning and returned a few moments later, complaining that she ate less than a bird and would never be her old self again at that rate.

By coffee time Marion was again present, well-kept but fragile, and with a bit more makeup than she used to use. That, too, was one of the details that bothered Harro. Did his mother know the cause of the decline that she was trying to mask with considerable care? And why did she go to all that trouble? For herself or for the people around her?

Maybe others were misled. He wasn't.

One morning, when Lucy had left for school and Reinier

had driven off in the direction of Dintelborg, Harro remained behind alone in the roomy, sunny dining room.

The oval table had become too big now that Inge, Charlotte, and Erik were out of the house, but things had once been different. Harro's thoughts went back fourteen, fifteen years, to the time when he and Rein had to bike six miles each day to the high school in Dintelborg.

He could see himself sitting down to a hasty breakfast, a book next to his plate, while Mother prepared lunches for him and Rein. She always did that herself, no matter how early they had to leave. Harro remembered how unreasonably angry he would become if Toos ever tried to take this task upon herself.

His brother didn't care at all; he just laughed at him. But Harro had always insisted that you could taste that Toos had no imagination. Her lunches were just like her: sober and good, but unattractive.

His father had told him that he should be ashamed. Toos did everything with so much love for them, and they did not show her nearly enough appreciation.

He had sulked as he listened, but in the quiet of his heart he knew that he was right: Mother's sandwiches tasted different. If he closed his eyes he could still see what she wore in the early morning hours: a bathrobe down to her toes, imprinted with gleaming white and yellow flowers that brought sunshine into the room. She wore no glasses in those days, and her hair was not yet done up, as it was later in the day; it hung loose around her neck, like a young girl's. He calculated how old she must have been in those days. About thirty-eight. That was still fairly young, as he now understood.

He realized all the more keenly how much he had always loved his mother. With concern he thought of the countless wrinkles that this past year had etched around her eyes, and he decided to arrange for a private conversation with his father that very afternoon.

At that very moment Marion lay with her eyes wide open, staring at the ceiling of her bedroom.

Her heart projected on it the faces of her children, one by one. Those of Inge and Bram, too, whom she had not seen in so many years. The little faces of her grandchildren, and finally the most trusted face of all, the powerful, furrowed face of Reinier, with the scar on the temple from a car accident and the heavy eyebrows above his clear, gray eyes that could look right through her.

She had promised him some time ago, after a visit to the doctor, that she would take things easier: sleep in in the morning, rest in the afternoon, early to bed in the evening. She kept to these rules, in part to satisfy Reinier, in part because she was so tired, so indescribably tired—every day a little more.

Now, after a week, she still felt how much the car trip to the airport had put her behind. But she said nothing to anyone.

She played along with the little game they played with her: Reinier, Lucy, and now Harro, too, who with extreme sensitivity to her needs deprived her of none of those things she had so enjoyed in her life—lively conversation at the table, full of humor and jest, the subtle teasing back and forth, the animated accounts of their day's experiences.

But behind all that carefree banter reposed a deep intimacy, a moving concern that had not remained hidden from her. Marion suspected what was the matter with her, but she felt the others already knew, at least Reinier and Lucy. The cheerfulness and flair with which they treated her each day had become, with her keen perceptiveness, a monument of bravery that often caused her to fight back tears in the loneliness of her room.

A few hours later on the same day, Harro stepped into his father's office unannounced.

Reinier was pleasantly surprised to see him there. Harro had never shown an interest in the factory.

"Aha! Did you come to see how things were going with the new expansion?" he asked with satisfaction, rising from his desk chair. "You came to the right place, Son. Sit down. Or did you come to see Rein? He is traveling today, I'm afraid."

Harro shook his head. He had not come for his brother. "No, it is good that I caught you alone. I wanted to speak with you, if it is not a bad time for you—with the business, I mean. Do you have a few minutes for me?"

Reinier demonstratively pushed aside his papers. "Always. Is something the matter?"

"I think so."

Harro looked his father directly in the eye and said without evasion, "It's about Mother. Don't think I have sand in my eyes. She is ill, isn't she?"

Reinier let his face sag. For a few seconds, a tense silence filled the room. Then he said, without emotion, "Yes, she is ill."

"Seriously ill," Harro pushed, but it was less a question than a statement of fact.

"Yes," his father said. He sat for a few moments lost in thought, but then he seemed to come to some sort of decision. "It is her spleen. Her blood is breaking down, and it makes her extremely tired. She is taking medication to slow the process as much as possible, but it cannot be stopped. Before too long she will need a blood transfusion, and then another, and then another." He made a helpless gesture with both hands. His mouth was a tight line of suppressed pain.

"How much longer?" Harro asked softly.

His father shrugged his shoulders. "A half year—maybe more, maybe less. I don't know."

"Why didn't you write me in Algeria about all this?"

"Your mother would not have wanted it. She wants nothing more than to keep the windows open to the sun for all of you. And I am prepared to respect that wish as long as possible. Not all of you children are alike."

For a brief moment an almost imperceptible smile danced across his drawn mouth. "You notice too much."

"Does Mother know?"

"Did you think she did?"

"You gave me that impression."

"No one has told her in so many words. The doctor spoke reassuringly to her about anemia in the transition years, but he does not know her as you and I know her. She knows most things by intuition, and I am convinced that she sees right through all that doctor talk."

"So the others still believe the fairy tale about anemia."

"All except Lucy. She has become my adjutant and confidante." There was grim pride in his words.

Harro reacted with shock. "But Father, she is not much more than a baby!"

"I know," Reinier said tiredly. "She is too young for such grief. But don't underestimate your little sister, Harro. She is the spitting image of her mother when she was a girl. She walks closer to God than any of us, and that gives her the inner strength to move mountains."

"I suspected from day one that she knew more than the others," Harro said, "but I was nearly sent on a goose chase by her exuberance and crazy ideas. You are acting so normally. You must forgive me for asking, Father, but how can you, in heaven's name, be so normal?"

He rested his forehead in the palm of his hand and thought about his mother as he had seen her that morning, with her soft blond hair curled against her neck.

"A half year—maybe more, maybe less," his father had said.

The grief of the coming farewell, which would be a permanent farewell, washed over him. The color left his face.

Reinier sat looking at him. A lump rose in his throat, but he said nothing, allowing his son the time to process this terrible thought.

After a while, Harro said hoarsely, "May I have a glass of water?"

Reinier poured one from the carafe on his desk. "I would like you to know that it was not I who placed this burden on Lucy. Of course I was the only one the doctor informed of the nature of Mother's sickness and the prognosis. I walked around alone with that revelation for a week, and I can assure you that it was the most miserable week of my life.

"But Lucy is just like you: She notices too much. One evening when I was really down, she came and sat on my knee and extracted my secret from me. 'Father,' she said calmly, 'if there is something wrong with Mother, then I ought to know. We are the only ones left at home; we must make a pact to help her. You just tell Lucy. Together we will be stronger.'

"She cried hard when she knew it all, but then she decreed that not a second more of this final year would be lost, not a second that can be used to make Mother happy.

"And it's strange, Harro. The things that make her happy are so simple: a cheerful atmosphere at home, a little animation and humor—all things that we can easily give her, if we want to."

"Easily?" Harro rebutted passionately. "Now that I know the situation, I would say that it is a difficult task you have given yourselves. If I, a full-grown man, will have great difficulty not weeping when I see Mother, then a seventeen-year-old girl might just as well hang it up, right? And you. You're only human."

"It is not always easy," Reinier admitted, "but it is our farewell gift to her, and that doesn't have to be cheap, Son."

Harro looked struck by that image. "Was that Lucy's idea?" His father nodded.

"I have indeed underestimated her," Harro confessed. He stood up. "I will gladly help, if it is within my power," he said simply.

They shook hands with painful force to reinforce their new understanding, then Harro left. He had forgotten the factory expansion, and even if he had remembered it, he would not have been able to muster any enthusiasm for it.

At the door he turned around.

"Oh, Father. One more thing. Would it be all right with you if I bring the girl whom I intend to marry to the Warbler next week?"

Reinier's face relaxed at this news. "The mysterious acquaintance from Nijmegen? Have you come to an agreement?"

"As far as I am concerned, there is not a shadow of a doubt," Harro said, "and I expect nothing but the best from it. Her name is Judith Uytenbogaard. I met her in Constantine."

"We will receive her with pleasure," his father said. "Your mother would like very much to see you happy."

❦ Chapter 9 ❧

When Harro visited Judith in Nijmegen for the second time, he invited her to spend her next free day in Borg.

She had not yet been able to find a new attitude toward him. There were moments when she was ready to give herself up, just as she was, but there were also moments when she suddenly was scared off by the consequences of her responsiveness and fell back into her reserved or defiant position.

Her reaction to his invitation, however, was very spontaneous. "Oh, yes," she reacted energetically, "that's right. I still have to take a look at that mysterious project of yours. I did more or less promise you that back in Constantine, didn't I?"

"*Promised* is maybe too big a word for it," Harro answered honestly, "but that does not diminish the fact that I have been counting on your coming to have a look."

"To tell you the truth, I am curious," she confessed. "But how do I get to Borg? I'm not exactly sure where it is. And will your parents understand if you suddenly show up with a female acquaintance?"

Harro looked at her from his place behind the wheel of the Chevrolet. She was sitting an unpleasant distance from him, at the farthest end of the front seat.

"So far my parents have shown more sympathy for my intentions than you have," he said smartly. "And as far as getting to Borg is concerned, you get there by car, since I will be picking you up."

"Who is the philanthropist who is always so willing to lend you his expensive sleigh?" she asked.

Harro laughed. "My very own father. Loyal, isn't he? But I will soon have to buy my own car, and it will certainly not be cut from the same cloth as this one, of that I assure you."

She looked around the luxurious car. "What does your father do, anyway?"

"He has a large leather factory in Dintelborg," Harro related. "I can't stand the place, but fortunately my brothers can. That is nice for my father, since at least now a successor is assured."

Judith was more impressed by the nonchalant mention of the factory than she was willing to let on. "You will have to be careful what you tell me," she said in jest, "or else I will end up taking you after all, for your money."

"For my father's money," he corrected lightheartedly.

"You don't seem to take the risk very seriously," she challenged.

"No," Harro said, "I don't. When you decide to marry me, you will do it first of all because you feel uprooted and are yearning to feel at home somewhere, not for riches or position. If you were counting on money, you would not have worked for four and a half years under the most difficult of circumstances for a pittance; and you definitely would not have gone into nursing."

"You certainly have an eye for my motives," she said, more or less shocked that he could see through her so well.

"And are you satisfied with that?"

"For the time being."

A pregnant silence fell between them.

Then Harro stated, "You have come to feel more for me than you thought possible. You are finding it difficult to keep your heart out of it."

She knew he was right. Already she had become entangled —with heart, soul, and mind—in the net he had spread for her with his constant affection, but she did not want to admit it until she was certain how he would react to her secret.

She silently scolded herself for not having told him back in Constantine of her broken wedding plans and the reason behind it. It would have been so easy back then; they were good friends and could have stayed that way, even if his intentions toward her changed.

The fact that nothing had yet been expressed and would therefore not have to be recalled, would have taken away the pain of any possible change of course.

But now everything was different. After their first kiss, their entire relationship entered a new dimension. By keeping her silence for so long, she unconsciously had led Harro into a moral dilemma.

This thought suddenly made her tired and subdued. It had all gone so fast. How could she have foreseen that what she saw as an innocent infatuation would so quickly take on such serious proportions?

She had not stayed out of range—on the contrary. She found herself involved in this affair with every fiber of her being, and that made her vulnerable and afraid. The rest of the evening she was noticeably quiet.

They rode around a bit and stopped for something to eat at the same restaurant.

Their conversation had many gaps, but Judith was buried so deeply in her own thoughts that over an hour had gone by before it sank in that he, too, was rather absent and more or less distracted.

She watched him, and the somber, concerned look in his eyes lifted her above her own problems for a moment.

She reflexively placed her hands on his. "You are so quiet, Harro. Is something the matter?"

"Yes," he said. "I received very bad news yesterday, and I can't get it out of my mind. I am sorry if I have been neglecting you." He told her about his mother's illness, and Judith recognized the symptoms.

"Leukemia," she said softly. "That's terrible, Harro. How old is your mother?"

"Just fifty-three."

"Still so young. I thought you had a sister of thirty-six."

"Yes, I do, but Inge is really our half-sister. She was born during my father's first marriage. This summer my parents were married for thirty years."

"The tone must be pretty subdued around your house right now," she assumed.

There was a quick, puzzling grin on Harro's lips. "Until you have met some of my housemates, I can't rightly describe the atmosphere around the house. You probably wouldn't understand. But *subdued* is not the right word."

"Your mother is a believer, isn't she?" Judith asked.

He nodded.

"That makes a big difference," she said earnestly. "But still, you will soon have to say good-bye."

Harro leaned somewhat closer to her. He had come up with an image that might clear up some of her puzzlement.

"We once celebrated a party that consisted of nothing but joy," he related. "It was the wedding of my sister Inge and Bram Dubois, shortly before they left for the interior of Suriname. It was an exclusive, well-organized party at which everyone was happy in spite of the fact that their upcoming departure hung over the party like a shroud.

"You can compare the tempered joy of that party with the way my mother now spends her days. Each new day is a precious gift that she takes with rapt attention."

"I have never heard anyone speak about someone who was about to die in that way before," Judith said with surprise. "You mother must be a remarkable woman."

Harro nodded. "That she is. But that makes it all the harder for us to let go of her."

"How is your father holding up?"

"Wonderfully. But I get the impression that he has not thought beyond the day on which she will leave us. The thought of the loneliness he will feel must be unbearable for him. Fortunately he is getting a lot of support from my little sister. Those two understand each other superbly. Father says that Lucy is the spitting image of Mother when she was young, and he would know."

Much later that evening, when Harro returned from Nijmegen and carefully drove the car into the garage of the Warbler, Marion awakened from her first sleep.

She lifted her head a little and looked to see what time it was.

Reinier, who had heard neither the car nor the garage door, was immediately alarmed by her slight movement. "What's the matter?" he asked urgently.

"Nothing," she said softly. "I just heard Harro come home."

Reinier thought of the girl in Nijmegen about whom Harro had spoken. It was good that something had come into his life to distract him from the blow he had taken the day before.

It was as though Marion read his thoughts. "Harro knows it now, too, doesn't he?" she asked in a whisper.

Reinier's body tensed. "What do you mean?" he asked sharply, grasping at the last miserable piece of straw in order to delay for a little while—just a little while—having to lay the cards on the table. Once it was put into words, the end of their happiness would seem closer and more unavoidable.

"That I will never recover," Marion said gently.

He took her in his arms in a tender, desperate gesture.

It made no sense to deny it, nor did he want to put a lie between them. "Why did you have to find out so soon?" he asked with pain. "We wanted so much to give you a few more months of undisturbed happiness."

He was defenseless under her soft, caressing hand.

"Reinier," she said, "I am a full-grown woman, not a child who can be brushed off. I can feel my own body, after all, and I do know something about the diseases that a person can get. We have always been honest with each other. What is it Reinier, leukemia?"

"Yes," he said helplessly.

They lay for a while, silently, next to each other, each wondering how to comfort the other.

While they lay there, they could hear their son downstairs locking the door and carefully making his way up the stairs. After he had closed his bedroom door behind him, Reinier asked softly, "How did you know about Harro?"

"I can't exactly put it into words. The way he looked at me; something indefinable in his attitude. I just knew, just as I knew from you and Lucy. Can I help it that those I love are an open book to me?"

Again they were quiet for a while.

Then Reinier asked, "Shouldn't the others be told now, too?"

"Inge," she said. "I would like so much to see Inge one more time. Would it be possible?"

"I will write her tomorrow," he promised.

"It will not be as difficult for Rein as for the others," she began again. "You can tell him."

It was a release to finally be able to say all the things that had been running through her mind recently.

"Rein has Paula and the children. For him the Warbler is no longer the center of the world. But Charlotte and Erik—I am worried about them, Reinier. They do not have the elasticity that Lucy and Harro have. They act very independent, but they both desperately need a home for spiritual support."

He knew that all too well. "I won't let them down, Marion," he said with difficulty.

He wanted so desperately to put her mind at ease, but he was fearfully aware of the fact that God would have to be at his side hour by hour if he was going to salvage the situation.

After all, what was he without her? He remembered all too well the time she was not there to bring beauty and order to his life. He had been a somber and bitter man, even in his youth. Would he have to return to such an existence for twenty or perhaps thirty years? Become old, sick, maybe even incapacitated—all without her?

His arms closed more tightly around her, and his hard-won self-control trickled away. "I can't live without you. I can't live without you," he whispered.

This was the moment Marion knew would have to come and which she had feared more than any other. She had, after weeks of internal struggle, made her peace with the fact that her time on this earth would soon be over, but for Reinier's sake her heart continually cried out to heaven, "Why?" No answer came.

She knew the depth of his grief and was all the more amazed at the courage with which he had silently borne her through this extraordinarily difficult time.

He had been strong, and that was good; but now he was weak, as anyone must from time to time be weak—even he.

Marion no longer resisted and buried her face in his shoulder, her tears flowing freely. With the knowledge that tomorrow would bring its own demands, it seemed a respite to be weak together.

❧ Chapter 10 ❧

At the entrance to the castle stood two stone pillars, between which had been hung a huge wrought-iron gate that always stood open. In the marble of the pillars, a name had been engraved with small, clear letters.

Harro brought the car to a stop in front of these pillars and silently watched Judith's reaction.

On this last leg of their journey from Nijmegen to Borg he began to tell her a few things about his work. He had described the properties he was managing and revealed something of his plans for those properties.

"Who owns it all?" she had asked.

"No one in particular. You have to look at it as belonging to a family."

"And that family has entrusted you with the management of that property and given you a free hand to modernize it and make it profitable again," she summarized. "Like a sort of estate manager, only with exceptional authority."

"You could put it like that," he agreed.

"You delight in it, don't you?"

"For more than twenty years now. When we turn that bend up there, you will be able to see the old house. You will notice it because the ivy is blood-red right now. As far as I am concerned, the castle is most beautiful this time of year."

The word *castle* struck something in her memory, although she could no longer remember precisely what.

And then came the bend, snippets of a breathtaking view, and the two pillars in front of which they had come to a stop.

"The House of Herewaarden," Judith read. It sent a shock through her to read his name on the pillars.

She looked at the ivy-covered walls of the old house and at the pointed towers rising against the light autumn sky.

The castle. Now she remembered the moment Harro had spoken of a castle. "You just tell her that you will soon be asked to marry a young nobleman and will go to live with him in a castle and will have everything that your heart desires."

It was the little tale that he gave to her to get the old woman she nursed off her back. But it was no little tale; she knew that now. This proud country palace belonged to his family. For a moment she felt she had been made a fool, but when she turned toward Harro, his grin was so disarming and sincere that her agitation melted away.

"So you are a nobleman," she concluded, a trace of disbelief in her voice.

"Indeed," he confessed with a smile. "But through no fault of my own, and if it's of any interest to you, I attach very little importance to it. The concept of nobility is nothing but a fantasy for me. We were always taught at home that true nobility can be found on all levels of society. Look over there."

He gently placed his hand against her neck and turned her head in the direction of the old house.

"What you see there is anything but fantasy. It is a piece of reality that has withstood the centuries and is more important than any title. I hope you can learn to love it, Judith."

It did not seem a difficult task to her.

For the sake of those strong, sensitive fingers that sent shiver after shiver down her spine, she was willing to accept any hut he offered her, let alone the historical gem that now rose before her.

She sat motionless under his touch, and Harro's voice continued, half-teasing, half-serious, close to her ear. "Although as the second-born son of my father I will not be able to bestow on you the title of baroness, which my grandmother used to go by, I must admit that from the very first time I met you I have seen you as the future lady of the House of Herewaarden. It is a shame that we have not kept the dresses from the time of the knights. Have I ever told you that you have an air of royalty about you?"

She blushed at his comment and reached a hand toward the door. "Silly!" she said, angrily and tenderly at the same time. "You and your romantic fantasies! Let me out, please!"

"You wouldn't run away, would you?"

"I'm not running away. But I wouldn't want you to pollute this Middle Ages scene with something as prosaic as a car. I want to walk from here and smell the grass and the trees and run through the fallen leaves."

Harro removed his hand from her neck and threw open the doors. "Agreed," he said with satisfaction. "You exceed my wildest expectations."

As they walked up the approach to the castle, Judith asked, "Who is living here now, Harro?"

"My uncle Diederick, a kind, old eccentric who is known in these parts simply as the squire, and to whom I have a great deal to be thankful for. My father and mother live about fifteen minutes from here in a villa called the Warbler, but that is a different story."

She sensed the warmth in his voice that was always present when he spoke about his family, and could imagine the affection was mutual.

It would be strange to have to share his attention with others who had a greater, or at least prior, claim to him.

They spent the remainder of the morning viewing the building, which had been restored countless times. Harro related for her stories and anecdotes from its history, and Judith continually prodded him on, because she found it pleasant to listen to his tranquil, animated voice.

In the portrait gallery she sought in vain for some resemblance between Harro and his ancestors.

Harro teased her mercilessly on that score. "What a delusion! The Van Herewaardens are all dark and handsome, with fiery eyes and broad shoulders. And here I am, blond and nearsighted, thin as a broomstick. I inherited everything from my mother's father, and he was bald on top of it all!"

She looked at him over her shoulder. "You have your own charm," she said, "and you know it very well."

"Oh, I do, do I?"

"You certainly make extensive use of it," she opined.

Then she turned her head once again and studied the portrait of the aged baroness.

Harro remembered how often he had been jealous of his robust older brother, who was the spitting image of his father, and how Inge once had comforted him with the words, "Don't be misled by Rein's popularity. We can't all be a copy of Father, and you have enough in your pack to develop your own personality in your own way."

Sweet Inge, she always seemed to know exactly what you needed.

They lunched with Diederick and Juliette in the west wing, and during the meal the past was once again the leading topic of conversation.

A bit overwhelmed by all these impressions, Judith let Harro lead her outside for a walk through the grounds. At the end of their amble, he brought her to a simple viewing tower.

"Have you saved enough energy to climb the tower?" he asked with a laugh. "If you get above the trees, you can see the Warbler. I promise you it is worth the effort."

A short time later he pointed out the house with the thatched roof dreamily nestled in a wreath of evergreens and late flowers.

"Now I have seen your entire kingdom," Judith concluded.

He nodded. "Would you like half?" he royally offered.

They both laughed, but Judith knew that although he spoke in jest, his words were another indication that he was seriously courting her to be his wife.

She knew that she could not keep putting him off indefinitely; he was too good to keep on a line. She pressed her nails into her palms and said with a voice breathless from the anxiety she felt, "I would love it, Harro, but first there is something I must tell you."

He did not make her confession easy.

It was as though he heard only her first five words. He turned toward her suddenly and laid his hands on her shoulders. All playfulness disappeared from his expression, and the eyes she saw so close to her own were the eyes of a man.

She felt herself grow weak under his glance.

" 'I would love it, Harro,' " he repeated quickly. "You said, 'I would love it, Harro.' Does that mean you want to be mine? Are you saying that you are giving me your trust?"

It struck her that he avoided the word *love,* still thinking of his promise not to force her feelings. Her trust was all he was asking of her. She nodded almost imperceptibly. "But I must first tell you something," she stubbornly persisted, with a sense of desperation.

"What is it?" he said, his mouth just above hers. "What is it that can't wait? Nothing that happened five years ago can ruin this moment."

He drew her close and kissed her as only he could. "I love you so much," he said, almost ashamed.

When he let her go, he saw that here were tears in her eyes.

He turned around and went and stood against the railing, his back to her. "As far as that fool from Wassenaar who left you in the cold is concerned," he said with threatening calm, "if you bore his child, just tell me."

A jolt went through her. Was that what he was thinking? "No," she cried, "no, no . . ."

If only it were that, she thought passionately.

Harro turned slowly toward her. "It rubs me against the grain that you continually dredge up your past humiliation, Judith," he said candidly. "Must you always insist on emptying your conscience? Do you think that I would love you less if I knew?"

For several seconds their eyes were locked in a stare.

She considered his last question and was convinced that she was giving the only possible answer when she haltingly said, "No, Harro, not you. Not you."

Again he pulled her to himself. "Well, then," he said, comforting her, "why don't we just forget the past and be happy?"

Judith stood absolutely still in the protective embrace of his arms. The temptation was so great. Why was she making it so hard for herself? She did not have to tell him. He had just said so himself.

He would not abandon her, of that she was certain. And what sense would it make under the circumstances to rein in his hopes for a glorious future this soon?

She should let him dream of a son who would someday take over the direction of his beloved domain. She should permit him this dream, at least for a time. The disappointment would come soon enough—but gradually, not as suddenly and painfully as it had been for her the last time.

It soon seemed more merciful and humane to spare him the truth, and she felt that an unbearable load had fallen from her and she was now, finally, in a position to respond to her heart.

The tension ebbed from her body, and Harro felt it like a liberation. Soon he would introduce her to his father and mother. He was a happy man.

❧ Chapter 11 ❧

A few days later, the old woman whom Judith had been nursing passed away. Judith remained another twenty-four hours in Nijmegen to assist the housekeeper with the various arrangements for the burial. Any further stay in that house of death was pointless and she was, due to circumstances, thrown back into her parental home.

She called Harro in Borg and told him she was planning to leave for her mother's home in Wassenaar the next morning.

He asked her not to take on any further nursing jobs, and his intentions were clear without further explanation: He wanted to marry as soon as possible.

She shared his longing—but to quit working so soon? "I'll have to see," she begged off, a bit impatiently. "I would not look forward to hanging around Wassenaar for several weeks."

Harro decided to drop the subject. "I was going to come to Nijmegen on Saturday," he said.

"Yes, you are going to have to drive a little farther now, but then you can meet my mother and Mr. Van Alkemade, too."

"You call him mister?" Harro interrupted with amusement.

"Yes! What did you think? Daddy? I would rather ... I don't get personal with strange men that quickly."

"Keep it that way," he advised, contented.

They talked a while longer about everything and nothing, and ended their conversation with a specific date for seeing each other again.

Judith arrived at home the following morning just about coffee time. She found her mother home alone; her stepfather was away on business.

He was a widower without children, and after their marriage had moved in with his new wife. Judith found very little changed at home, as far as furnishings were concerned.

But the atmosphere had definitely changed. She was, however, realistic enough to realize that she was in part the reason for that.

Mrs. Van Alkemade immediately poured coffee for her daughter, and they conversed about the death in Nijmegen.

Then Judith blurted out, "I am going to be married shortly, Mother."

Her mother was struck dumb. "Married?" she finally asked. "To whom?"

"To an engineer with whom I became acquainted in Algeria. His name is Harro Van Herewaarden, and he comes from Brabant. You spoke with him by telephone not too long ago; maybe you remember. If you had not given him my address that time, he probably never would have found me. Thanks for your help."

Mrs. Van Alkemade was a little taken aback by the cynical undertone in her daughter's voice. "If you love the man enough to marry him, why didn't you give him your address yourself?" she asked insightfully.

Judith gave her an odd look. "You know why. But I'll tell you, anyway. I wanted him to have a family of his own, so I withdrew."

"And now?"

"He appears to want to marry me regardless. I have come to that conviction the last few weeks. And if he is prepared to marry me at any cost, who could blame me for not letting this chance slip by?"

"Then he knows," Mrs. Van Alkemade probed.

"No," Judith said, provoked. "No, he does not know. I have tried to tell him twice, but he does not seem to want to know. He always tries to stop me. He is a fool. A sweet, impractical, noble fool."

Her lips began to quiver, she laid her head on her arms and cried. "I love him," she choked.

She heard her own voice say the three words, and she suddenly felt very calm. Did she really love him? She must, in light of the fact that everything inside her resisted causing him any grief.

Simply because of the uninhibited, spontaneous love for life with which he was able to take the simplest things and turn them into a celebration, she had fallen in love with him. Unsettled by the intensity of her feelings, she realized that she was prepared to lie and deceive if she could thereby ensure his carefree happiness.

Mrs. Van Alkemade sat gazing at her daughter for a time, as she slowly regained her composure.

She felt it was her place to give advice and support, but she had never been able to communicate well with Judith.

"He must know, my child," she finally said, timidly. "You have a moral obligation to tell him. Shall I . . . ?"

Judith dried her tears. It was as though a mask had fallen before her face, and her mother knew that all avenues toward an intimate conversation were now closed.

"You will do nothing," she said firmly. "I will take care of this myself when the time is right, and I ask you please not to interfere or allude to it when Harro is here. After all, I did not interfere with your marriage," she added with spite.

Her mother blinked her eyes at that gibe. "Darling," she pleaded, "I know very well that it is not easy for you to see someone else in your father's place. But I was so alone, so terribly alone at the time. Before I was even fifty years old, my life appeared to have no meaning. Papa was dead, you were so far away. I couldn't take it alone anymore. You must understand that? No one knows better than I do that a second marriage has its dark side," she finished, rather sadly.

Judith felt ashamed for her outburst. She took her mother's hand. "I am sorry, Mom," she said remorsefully. "You mean well, but we must each solve our own problems: you yours and I mine."

Not another word was exchanged between the two women on the question.

Judith did, however, at her mother's request, fill in some of the details of her engagement: where and how she met Harro, what his family was like, where they would live for the time being.

By the time he came on Saturday, Mrs. Van Alkemade already had formed a fairly precise picture of him.

Harro did not have the slightest difficulty feeling at home in the new environment. Nor had Judith feared such; she was aware of his ability to get along with people.

He had come to Wassenaar in his own new car, about which he had consulted with Judith.

He found an eager audience in Judith's stepfather, who loved mechanical things, as he summed up the many qualities of his new acquisition. The two soon had their heads under the hood, carrying on an extensive conversation about the pros and cons of various different types of motors, to which Judith and her mother listened with amusement.

In the afternoon Harro and Judith took a drive to the beach, where they parked the car so they could walk by the sea. November was living up to its reputation: the hard wind that conjured a white head on each wave lent the sea a wild beauty.

Windswept and with cold hands, they returned to the deserted parking lot.

Once back in the car, Judith straightened out her hair. Harro then rubbed her hands until they glowed. She felt happy and relaxed; the few hours in his presence had wiped away days of restlessness.

Everything will happen as it must, she was now able to think. *The most important thing is that we want the best for each other.*

When the blood was circulating through her fingers again, she threw her arms around his neck with an impulsive gesture and, for the first time, kissed him on her own initiative.

"Thanks for your good work, Harro," she said gratefully. "I am completely unthawed again." The car remained parked on the lot for some time, a warm island in a cold gray sea of concrete.

Harro was the first to comment on how late it was. "There must be something wrong with my watch," he said, grabbing her wrist to compare watches. "Somehow we lost an hour."

"There is nothing wrong with your watch," Judith teased. "It must be us."

"You," he corrected. "You are much too sweet. Why didn't anyone warn me that you could be so sweet?"

He started the car. "If we hurry, we can still be in Wassenaar before the stores close," he said. "Then I can still buy you a little present."

"But it is not my birthday."

"I don't need a reason to spoil you," he assured her.

He stopped the car in front of a row of shops, and they mingled with the late Saturday afternoon crowd swarming the street, where all the lights had already been turned on.

From the elaborate display at the jeweler's, Harro chose a bracelet for her, which he immediately placed around her wrist.

When they were outside again, she placed her arm through his, and he knew everything was all right between them.

They had gone but a few steps when a shock of emotion ran through Judith's body. A little farther down the street she saw the Scheppers family.

There was no way to avoid the painful confrontation. She saw all four of them at the same time: Jan Willem, his wife, and two small children—a boy of about two years in white boots and a daughter in a stroller.

Harro sensed the short, hard jolt that ran through her, although he was not able to discern who had unsettled her, since the street was full of people. But he intuited that it had something to do with the reason she had fled Wassenaar years ago.

Of course he had often wondered what it was that had happened in her life years ago, and now that question forced its way to the surface. He was hedging his bets that it was an affair with a married man, a scandal that had dragged her good name through the mud. But it was so long ago that it was unreal to him. Judith was Judith. Whether she had made moral mistakes or was upstanding, he desired to know nothing.

What mattered to him was the fact that she had experienced a lot of grief, and he wanted nothing more than to heal the wound life had dealt her as quickly and completely as possible.

When he felt the jolt run through her, he reacted immediately by pulling her closer to himself. "Hold on tight," he whispered from the corner of his mouth, playing on her pride. "Let them see what you are worth."

Somehow she managed to greet them with the composure of a grand lady and to continue walking a few steps with an air of nonchalance as the solidly built man who approached them rather nervously tipped his hat.

But once they had passed, Harro felt her tremble.

"Calm down, sweetheart!" he implored.

"That was Jan Willem," she said, as though to explain everything.

She had never before mentioned his name to Harro.

But she knew that the reappearance of the man who was once her fiancé did absolutely nothing for her. It was his children that had shaken her so. That little boy with his white boots, and that little girl with her blond curls. Never had she desired a child as she did at that moment.

But her arms would remain empty—her womb, her arms, and her home—and never would she be at peace with that thought.

"You're shaking like a leaf," Harro said. "What does that man still mean to you, Judith?"

"Nothing. Nothing—absolutely nothing!" she answered fervently. "He couldn't hold a candle to you."

He believed her, although he knew that something did not ring true.

It was quiet between them for a few moments.

His mind sought an explanation for her desperation, but found none. Then he accepted the mystery and gave up the guessing game.

Once at the car, he took her trembling hands in his own.

"This will not happen again, Judith," he said with authority. "In less than three weeks I am taking you away from here. We will get married in Brabant."

❧ Chapter 12 ❧

Of the three weekends before the marriage would be performed at Dintelborg's city hall and confirmed in the old village church of Borg, Judith spent two at the Warbler.

There was much to be arranged and to talk over. They desperately needed the time.

It did from time to time cause some agitation that Harro was proceeding so quickly with his wedding plans, but he was not about to let himself be swayed on this matter.

With his parents there was little resistance to overcome. They had, after all, not had opportunity to form anything but a fleeting impression of the woman he had chosen, but that was accompanied by an almost infinite trust in his insight.

When he had confronted them with the fact that within three weeks they would be one daughter-in-law richer, Reinier had frowned. "Isn't that rather head over heels, Son?"

"Listen, Father," Harro said decisively, "since my days as a student I have known neither hearth nor home. Every week

I traveled back and forth between Borg and Wageningen—for seven years, if we count the time that I was in the military. Then there were my tour of America and the endless months in Algeria. I hope you can muster some understanding for the fact that I would like to settle down and am yearning to drop anchor. I can't bear the thought of spending another winter of weekends traveling back and forth. And for Judith, that is even more the case. She has no place to call home anymore, now that an unfamiliar man lives in her mother's home."

"We fully understand your desire to begin your own family," his father answered, "but our only reservation is that you have known each other for such a short time. Can you two already be so sure of your feelings?"

"When you had known Mother for five months," Harro asked strategically, "did you know what you were getting in her? Yes or no?"

Marion laughed softly and exchanged a knowing glance with the two men.

"Okay, okay," Reinier said. "I give up."

Shortly thereafter Marion went to the hospital in Dintelborg for her blood transfusion. She insisted on it.

She would so desperately need the temporary energy in the coming weeks, first in order to take part in Harro's wedding, but also so she could, for the last time, give the December holidays something of their old shine.

Recently she had frequently thought that she was in fact more fortunate than many who are taken suddenly from life. She had been allowed to say an intimate farewell to each and every thing, to have at least one more confidential talk with all of her children and build for them more beloved memories to leave behind.

Reinier brought her to the hospital.

He was controlled, but very quiet, nor did Marion have

much to say, yet they each knew what was in the heart of the other.

Since Marion had become ill, they had been in tune with each other more than ever before, and the personal contact that had always been considerable became even more intense—to the point of sensing nearly every silent wish and the slightest variation in tone.

When they arrived at the hospital, Marion realized how healthy she had been until recently. The last time she had been admitted here as a patient was more than thirty years before.

The building had been renovated twice and expanded since then, but the new wing stood behind the old, where the garden had once been. The facade had retained the same appearance over the years.

Before she got out, she slipped her arm through Reinier's. "Do you still remember when I had appendicitis?" she asked.

He looked at her and nodded. "I have far too many memories of this old building," he said grimly. "And not many of them are pleasant."

She understood.

His first wife had died here after a prolonged and horrible battle with death, and several years later he had himself lain in a room in this old building, tottering on the brink of death after a serious car accident.

Erik and Lucy had also been here with serious concussions, and Charlotte with a dangerous bout of blood poisoning.

Together they summed up the grief and worry they had experienced within these walls over the course of the years. But at the same time they knew that none of that had weighed on them so heavily as what brought them here on this day: the assumption of a lost battle against a gradually encroaching death that could not be defeated, only accepted.

Out of an irrepressible desire to find something positive to balance the painful burden resting on them, Marion said, with defiance in her voice, "We have almost forgotten something, Reinier. Both of Paula and Rein's children were born here."

She felt the aching press of his fingers.

"Birth, life, death," he said wearily. "The eternal cycle. But no one wants it, Marion."

"And yet," she said stubbornly, "death does not have the last word."

"I know," he conceded. "But we don't learn very quickly when we are older. In spite of the irrefutable fact that God has promised us a new heaven and a new earth, we still cling with both hands to this beloved, old, evil world where we have been so happy together. You must feel that way, too, sweetheart?"

She lifted her face toward him. "We will live on through our children, Reinier," she said soothingly. "Long after we are gone, Van Herewaardens will still be alive who owe their existence to our love."

Her stay in the hospital was short. On Friday she returned to the Warbler a completely new woman. She looked so deceptively well after the transfusion that Charlotte, having arrived in a panic from Rome, refused to believe that what her father had written was true.

As long as Marion was with them, Charlotte was able to control herself, but once alone with her father, she stomped about like a child in powerless anger.

"The doctors must be wrong, Father! She has never looked so good!"

Reinier smiled sadly. "If you had been here last week, you would speak differently, Charlotte. And in six weeks this recovery will probably be lost. Don't deceive yourself with false hopes. Try to accept the fact that she will not get better again, as the rest of us have."

"You mean nothing can be done for her?"

"Of course. We can make her departure easier by being loving and courteous toward one another and by not losing our courage. Then she can close her eyes with a heart at rest."

The next day the house was as filled as it had been in previous years.

Harro and Judith were there. Erik had returned from Rotterdam, and now that Charlotte was home again, Rein and Paula wanted to stop by to say hello.

Toos was in her glory with all the busyness. She cooked pan after pan of food and put out pot after pot of coffee and tea, which were served by Lucy and Judith.

Marion, freed from the constant exhaustion she had carried around with her like a load of lead, was once again the happy nucleus of her family.

She had for each and every one an intense and eager interest and worked heart and soul on the plans for the upcoming wedding.

Judith understood that the *savoir vivre* of this woman and her inner strength had in no small way contributed to the fact that Harro was the master at living that he incontestably was.

Marion, gifted with a vitality to which she was no longer accustomed, did not want this day to end. Before she retired for the night, she went to her daughters' room, as she had so many times before. She tucked Lucy in and kissed her blond hair. The communication between them was so great that they needed few words to express their feelings.

"Good night, my little lovely. Sleep well."

"Good night, Mama. It was a special day, wasn't it?"

With Charlotte it was more difficult.

"Mother," she said with quivering lips. "Mother, I don't want to cry. They are all so awfully brave here. They will despise me for it."

Marion shook her head and pressed Charlotte's head to

her breast. "Everyone here cries when she has to, and you may, too, my child. But mind you, the Warbler is not a house of mourning. Those who know that they are going to God may be happy until their very last day here on earth. Isn't it a privilege that we as a family live in that thought?"

The next day Paula called and asked for Harro. She and Rein were going to spend Sunday evening with friends, but their baby-sitter had suddenly canceled. She asked whether he and Judith might not be inclined to step into the vacancy.

"With pleasure," he answered without a second thought. "You just go and have a good time, girl, and don't hurry back. What time do you want us there?"

"Eight-thirty is early enough," Paula said. "I think you're wonderful, Harro!"

"I think you are wonderful, too." He returned the compliment with a sunny laugh. "Good-bye, Paula. See you tonight."

"That sounds like a date," Judith said, just coming up.

He turned toward her. "I was just exchanging compliments with my sister-in-law."

"Oh?"

"You certainly can't be jealous of her?" he asked, amused.

"Of course," she said. "How can I help it?"

That evening she could not help but remember this little exchange.

Paula let them into the brightly lit hallway of the little house. Rein was just leaving one of the rooms, pulling on his overcoat at the same time. "My wife really arranged this one nicely for you, didn't she?" he asked with satisfaction. "You two no doubt have a lot to talk over privately, and it is like a beehive at home at the moment. Here you can have some quiet—at least if her majesty the baby cooperates," he smirked.

"I already told Paula that she was wonderful on the telephone," Harro answered.

"We were also young once," Paula remarked indulgently, and her brother-in-law had her immediately in a neck lock.

"How old are you anyway, little girl?" he teased. "Twenty-four years old counting on both hands? You're still wet behind the ears!"

The quick, slender woman tried to escape his grasp.

"Rein, help me!" she demanded. "Your brother doesn't seem to understand that he must treat a mother of two children with the proper respect!"

Rein smiled. "Harro, leave my wife alone," he declared authoritatively, in order to say, with the obvious pride of a father, to Judith, "Would you like to see our progeny before we go?"

She could not elude his invitation and followed him to the children's room.

Little Reinier slept sideways in his crib in a plump, blue-striped pajama, but little baby Pauline lay with wide-open eyes in her pink cradle.

For a moment Judith felt that it was completely futile to have evaded the children of Jan Willem. These little Van Herewaardens plunged the same stake into her heart. Yes, she was jealous of Paula—but in a different way from anything Harro could imagine.

Only later in the evening did her sense of well-being return.

❧ Chapter 13 ❧

Immediately after the wedding, which for the sake of Marion's health would be kept small and quiet, Judith and Harro intended to move into the House of Herewaarden.

As they spent the evening at Rein's and Paula's, Harro asked her where she would like to spend the honeymoon.

"In Borg," she promptly replied.

He laughed. "Are you serious?"

"Of course. I have seen more than enough of the world for the time being, Harro. And what about you? You have barely begun with your work. You certainly don't want to be somewhere on the French Riviera; you want to be walking over your fields and talking with the tenant farmers. You want to implement your plans, put people to work, and come home in the evening to your own wife."

He sat for a time looking at her with a quizzical expression.

"Am I not right?" she wanted to know.

"Of course. You see right through me. But I would never

have said it myself. I would not have wanted to deprive of you of the romance which is, strictly speaking, your due."

Her eyebrows went up. "You will still make good and sure that the romance is not neglected; of that I can assure you."

They frolicked a bit, but then Judith became serious. "In light of everything," she said, "you should stay near your mother as long as she is still in good health, Harro. We can always travel later."

Her understanding pleased him, and he considered it an advantage that she—with her disturbing cynical outlook on so many things—could muster the willingness to enhance the atmosphere of love and togetherness in the home of his parents.

Even Judith was well aware of her change in disposition. She had initially, out of habit, braced herself against the new milieu, but she soon realized that the mistrust was coming completely from one side—hers.

Through the totally natural, unforced way in which she had been accepted into the circle, she felt disarmed and in a strange, still somewhat skittish way, she felt solidarity with the others.

In the meantime, the plans for the near future continued to take on fixed form. They would inhabit a number of rooms in the eastern wing of the House of Herewaarden, opposite the wing in which Diederick and Juliette lived.

The middle part of the castle was by far and away the oldest. In it were found, among other rooms, the main hall and the portrait gallery. An ancient spiral staircase, adorned with carvings from the Middle Ages, led out of the wide, tiled hall to the upper levels.

The two wings, which had not been added until the eighteenth century, were much better suited for comfortable living than the older portion of the castle.

Judith wandered with Harro through the available rooms,

where all the sheets and dustcovers had been removed just for the occasion. Although they had the entire wing at their disposal, neither of them felt it necessary to make use of more than four rooms for their daily living.

Finally they made their choice.

Judith gazed at the silver place settings, the linens, the porcelain, the Chinese pottery and crystal. It made her dizzy, strange as it was, living in a house where she would only gradually get to know her way around, a house full of furniture and other fixtures that did not belong to her, nor strictly speaking to Harro—things that piece for piece were lovely and expensive, but not yet familiar or her own.

"Would you rather have a modern little house, like Paula?" Harro asked, as though divining her thoughts.

He stood in a deep shadow as he spoke. A dark stained-glass window stood behind him, and an ancient crown streamed in muted tones around his blond head.

A knight without armor, flitted through her head, and she knew that that was the last thing she wanted; to deprive him of his beloved historic backdrop.

This was at least one place where she would not have to stand in the way of his happiness.

How strange the atmosphere seemed to her at that moment, with all the different eras of furniture that she could only with difficulty begin to identify. But as long as Harro was by her with his self-assurance and élan, she would certainly not be unhappy here.

"A modern little house like Paula?" she repeated his question. "If that means that I have to trade you in for Rein, I'll pass."

He grinned, relieved. "What do you have against Rein?"

"Nothing. But I am just beginning to like you."

She escaped his grasp.

". . . and you are really in your element here," she added over her shoulder.

A little later they talked over some of the practical details and alterations while sitting in lovely Louis XIV chairs that were plushly upholstered in scarlet and gold.

Harro laid his hand on hers. "It is all going so fast," he said apologetically. "We will just have to get by here for the time being, and you must remember that you have an entire winter ahead of you to set everything up as you think best."

"You mean it is not a sacrilege to change things around here?" she asked with a general gesture to the surroundings.

Harro laughed heartily. "Darling," he said, "you are at home here, not in a museum! I'll even go one step further: I insist that you make at least one room modern, with plain walls and contemporary furniture, a television set and, as far as I am concerned, a Picasso on the wall. Although I deeply admire what my ancestors have acquired, I would still like a place in my home that is contemporary and in which I can recognize your tastes."

Her eyes began to glaze over.

"Aren't you concerned that it will ruin the atmosphere?" she protested, as a mere formality.

"Do you see the chairs we are sitting in?" Harro asked. He knocked on the arm and said nonchalantly, "These chairs were made around 1680 by a cabinetmaker in Brussels upon the request of a certain Cecilia Van Herewaarden. She was a unique young woman who had been married but a short time to my great-great-great-grandfather. He was named *Reinier,* probably, since almost all of them were named *Reinier.*

"This Cecilia was tired of having to sit on the hard old seats belonging to her husband's family. She wanted modern furniture, and her youthful husband, who was as crazy about her as I am about you, said immediately, 'You go ahead and do it!'

99

"But her mother-in-law, who was called Machtheld and was a domineering woman, would hear nothing of this modern paraphernalia. At that time the House of Herewaarden was still completely in its medieval glory, and Cecilia's things, made in the style of the French, found no mercy in her eyes. They ruined the atmosphere."

Judith ran a careful finger along the tasteful ornamentation. "Those things have held up pretty well in other respects," she said dryly.

He nodded, laughing. "Every style of furniture you see here was modern at one time, Judith Uytenbogaard," he said, summarizing his tale, "and you have as much right as the beautiful Cecilia of yesteryear."

Judith was greatly amused by his story.

She suddenly viewed all the old fixtures with new eyes, now that she realized that young, lively people laughed, fought, and suffered among them. Nevertheless, she had the suspicion that the story had risen from Harro's vivid imagination.

But after they were married, when she checked his story out with Diederick, it all turned out to be true. The names, the dates, even the bill of sale for the Louis XIV chairs could be documented.

Once Diederick was on his hobby horse, he gave her free access to the family records and pointed out to her the famous Cecilia, who later became the mother of five children, of which three died at a young age of smallpox.

The conversation with Diederick, who had also tutored Harro in these things, was very interesting to Judith.

"May I return, Uncle Diederick?" she asked. "I would like to know everything about the family history, and someday I will score some points with Harro."

She could not have pleased him more.

The winter passed more quickly than she had imagined. In the servants' quarters of the castle a couple lived—the

Van Dongens—who had for years been in charge of the up-keep of the unused portions of the castle.

Mrs. Van Dongen, a robust forty-year-old woman, held her own. She continued to maintain the lion's share of the house-work in the newly created situation, but Judith had insisted on cooking herself. She did that with great pleasure, and everyone assured her in jest that as far as that was concerned, there were a lot of points to earn with Harro.

Harro had little time for her during the day, but she was never bored. In addition to the extraordinary history lessons she was receiving in Diederick's sitting room, she was also learning to drive. She went for driving lessons a couple of times a week in Dintelborg, on Harro's insistence.

She also frequently popped in at the Warbler in order to keep her mother-in-law company, usually at times when Reinier was at work and Lucy at school.

They had several intimate conversations and one day, when Marion confided to her that she was not looking forward to the day she would not be able to take care of herself and would have to rely on the help of strangers, Judith spontaneously offered, "You won't have to take on a strange nurse. If you would like, I will take care of you as long as you are able to stay home."

"Will I . . ." Marion hesitated for a moment. Her voice trembled. "Do you think I will have to go to the hospital in the end?"

This was a question with which she did not want to trouble Reinier, even though it had been on her mind for a long time. One of the last wishes she secretly harbored was to die at home.

She had had her third blood transfusion now, and she knew that she was regressing. Judith knew it, too, and did not deny it.

"That is normally the case," she answered carefully, "but

maybe provisions can be made. Would you like me to take that up with Father, or with the doctor, if I run into him?"

Marion gave a silent nod.

Judith reflected on how easily she had accepted Harro's father as her own, while at the same time having had so much trouble accepting Mr. Van Alkemade.

Immediately after the wedding, Harro had begun to address his parents-in-law as *Father* and *Mother,* and he had demanded that she do the same, even though her stepfather did not have her complete sympathy.

"You are hurting your mother by consciously maintaining the distance," he had said, more assertively than she was accustomed to, "and you are yourself responsible for the fact that he views you not as a grown-up daughter, but as a stubborn young woman."

Judith yielded to his urging, just as she had yielded to his influence in so many other matters, resistantly, but nevertheless recognizing the wisdom of his decisions.

The longer she was with him, the more she conformed to his way of life. There was very little left of the recalcitrant Judith who was accustomed to going her own way without any scruples.

In the back of her mind was the indelible knowledge that she was in Harro's debt. By being pliant to his wishes in everything, she had the feeling that she was able to pay back that debt a little. She was becoming proficient at the art of setting aside unpleasant thoughts, and she frequently succeeded for days, indeed weeks at a time, in enjoying the happiness that had been so incomprehensibly dropped into her lap.

Living with Harro seemed to be an unending adventure.

He was an inexhaustible reservoir of surprises, such as the silly, delightful night walk he led her on when the first snow fell and he, awakening in the middle of the night, immediately lost his heart to the fantasy world outside.

Life with him was an exciting adventure; not the least because of the inimitable way he was able to predict her yearnings. In these moments she was completely defenseless against his alluring, exotic tenderness, and she found it incomprehensible that there had been a time when she more or less looked down on him as still wet behind the ears.

There were also other moments, however, moments when her mother's instinct played tricks on her.

That was the case when he had been at the Warbler and divulged to her his grief over Marion. She comforted him as though he were her own little boy, and it made their intimacy even deeper and more valuable that he was not ashamed to repose in her arms from time to time, weak and sad. So the winter passed.

And then Inge came.

❧ Chapter 14 ❧

At the mission post deep in the interior of Suriname, the mail was not delivered daily.

On the contrary, only at set times was an expedition put together for the ascent to the Saramacca River. The slender dugout canoes, the only means of transportation capable of surviving the numerous rapids, when manned by an extremely qualified native crew, were always greeted with jubilation upon their arrival.

They brought, in watertight cases, all the needs of the post: instruments for the hospital ordered long before, medicine, utensils, and a number of other things, among them the mail—packages and letters from friends in Paramaribo and family in Holland.

Many weeks after it was mailed, Inge and Bram Dubois received the long letter written to them by Reinier in which he alerted them to Marion's wish to see Inge once more before she died.

This letter created a great deal of unrest at the settlement. In addition to the grief caused by the dire news and the desire to grant Marion's dying wish if possible, an infinite number of practical details loomed before them to be resolved.

Although Reinier expressly promised to pay all costs that might arise as a result of a visit to the Netherlands, there were so many other problems.

Inge was indispensable in the hospital; she was the only surgical nurse available to Bram. If she were to be absent for an extended period of time, it would be like losing his right hand, since none of the native nurses, no matter how adroit or willing, were able to take over her duties.

They agreed that a replacement would have to come from Paramaribo to take her place temporarily.

But how would they be able to find a qualified nurse on such short notice who would be willing to take on the difficult journey to the interior in order to bury herself in the wilting heat of the jungle for several weeks?

And then there were the children. They had four: Jaques, Marie-Louise, Reina, and Marion. The older three were already of school age. The boy was eleven, and the two girls nine and six.

Inge was in the habit of giving them their elementary education a few hours each day. They were healthy, well-tempered children, well schooled in the dangers of their environment, who spoke the language of the natives as fluently as they spoke Dutch, the language spoken at home.

Bram and Inge were not deeply concerned about them. They would no doubt overcome the temporary absence of their mother.

But the youngest, the one they called little Marion and who was just over a year, was the focus of all the family concerns.

She struggled with serious digestive problems and was barely able to cope with the climate of the jungle.

Bram had in silence made a diagnosis hundreds of times, but did not dare reveal it to Inge. The solution also raised resistance in his own heart: The baby would have to leave them.

Finally, when a replacement for Inge had indeed been found and the plans for Inge's departure were already advanced, he ventured raising the subject with Inge.

"Wouldn't you like to take little Marion with you to the Netherlands?"

"In order to make things worse than they already are?" Inge reacted fiercely. "With that terrible journey that I hardly dare undertake myself, with strange foods, drastic changes in temperature. It could kill her!"

"It could also save her," he gently corrected.

She looked him in the eye for a long time before it finally dawned on her what he was suggesting.

"Leave little Marion in Holland?" she cried in disbelief. "I won't do it, Bram. I will never do it! I can't be without her!"

"I know the thought frightens you," he said tenderly, "but maybe it simply has to be done, sweetheart, precisely because we can't be without her."

Inge began to cry. "The only person I might have been willing to entrust her to would have been Mother," she said between gasps, "but Mother is dying, Bram." Her tears became ever more abundant.

He caressed her long black hair and did not push it any further.

"Will you take good care of my baby when I am gone?" she finally asked.

"I will look after her myself," he promised earnestly. "No one else will take my place."

"Except Marie-Louise," she smiled through her tears.

They both thought tenderly of their oldest daughter, who was already becoming a little mother for her baby sister and had relieved Inge of a number of duties.

It was spring before she was finally on her way.

When they had put the mountainous region with its many rapids behind them, the modern world began to manifest itself. The last stage of the journey, which twelve years before she had made with her husband in the opposite direction by boat, was now made by plane.

In the city she stayed for a few days with a colleague of Bram's and made the most urgent purchases in order to bring her wardrobe somewhat up-to-date.

Then, once again through the air, she made the longest but most comfortable leg of her long journey from the airport in Paramaribo to the Netherlands.

Reinier met her at Schipol International near Amsterdam.

At home her arrival was looked forward to with great anticipation. Ever since it had been made known that she would indeed be coming, Inge became a frequent topic of conversation at the Warbler and in the village.

For many of the residents of the village who had participated in their wonderful wedding, Bram and Inge Dubois had become more or less legendary figures.

Also in the House of Herewaarden, Inge's arrival was celebrated, even though the reason for it was a cause of grief.

The morning of the day of her arrival, Judith asked at breakfast, "Tell me again what Inge was like when she was younger, Harro."

"She was a wonderful sister, and exceptionally pretty," he complied.

Judith knew the portrait of Inge that hung in the sitting room of Bram's parents' home. Many times she had admired the fine features of her unknown sister-in-law and felt coarse and drab by comparison.

She wrinkled her eyebrows. "Was?" she repeated. "Isn't she any more?"

"You can't burn the candle at both ends and expect it to stay the same," Harro answered. "When I visited them two years ago I was shocked—by Inge, but also by Bram. Their youth is definitely gone. They have both acquired a certain tawny quality, but also something intangible, unaffected by age or fashion. A sort of universal worthiness. No one who meets Inge now will immediately say, 'What a beautiful woman,' but will say, 'This is a woman of character.' And that goes for Bram, too."

"Did she also study medicine?"

"Oh, yes. She finished her schooling shortly before Bram and she became engaged. Then she broke off her program and took courses in surgical nursing. Bram was almost finished with his residency in surgery, and they complemented each other perfectly."

Judith hoped that she would have plenty of opportunity to exchange thoughts with Inge during her stay in the Netherlands. What she had heard about life on the mission post intrigued her very much.

She did, after all, know from her own experiences the difficulties confronting doctors and nurses when treating patients in a primitive country.

Bram and Inge also undoubtedly had had many depressing experiences in the course of the years. Where did they find the strength to continue rowing against the current for so many years, the staying power to remain steadfast while only difficult and minuscule advances were made?

She posed the question with some hesitation to Harro.

He looked puzzled. "But you were in the same boat for years. If anyone would know, it would be you."

She shook her head. "Inge and Bram went into the jungle with the conscious intention of helping and serving," she said with something of her old bitterness, "but with me it was so different. I just wanted the farthest corner of the world to crawl to, like a dog that had been kicked."

It had been a long time since she had openly alluded to the humiliation she had undergone.

Her comment aroused the same sudden anger in his eyes that she had noticed at the beginning of their acquaintance.

He could not bear the thought that someone had been in a position to wound her in such a way that the memory still pained her after all these years.

He pushed his chair back and walked around the table. Standing behind her, he laid his hands on her shoulders.

"Judith," he asked, hurt, "why can't you forget? What did they do to you that makes it impossible for you to forget?"

Her heart seemed to stand still for a moment.

The moment had again presented itself to lay her cards on the table—and again she let it go by.

Too many half lies between them blocked the way to the truth.

She sensed from the tension in his hands that he was still expecting an answer.

"You didn't want to know," she said softly, while despising herself for her cowardice.

The press of his fingers ebbed away. "You're right," he said stiffly. "I'm sorry."

He pulled on his raincoat and went about his work with his usual farewell, but Judith suffered the entire day from the painful reserve of his apology.

❧ Chapter 15 ❧

Spring broke through with a swiftness that caught every-one by surprise. A few sun-filled days were enough to coax all the fruit trees to release their blossoms.

Marion had grown so weak that she had to spend nearly the entire day in bed. Blood transfusions were needed, one after another. Her arms were bruised from the constant injections needed to slow the breakdown of her blood.

Every morning Judith came to help her and then would sit on her bed for hours at a time, bathing in the peace emanating from the other.

On one of these mornings, Harro unexpectedly entered the room with an armful of blossoming branches. It was a very unusual time for him to visit, and Judith blushed at this abrupt meeting. Since their strange, intense conversation of a few days before, their happiness seemed less spontaneous than it had before.

Harro hardly looked at her. All his attention was focused

on Marion. "Pear blossoms, Mother," he said fondly, "and plum and peach, and—look here—wild cherry. All from the castle garden. We could never pick them before, remember? But now I am the boss, and I picked out the most beautiful branches for you."

The bed was buried under the white wealth of flowers, and here and there a hint of pink. The blossoms lay scattered in random extravagance against the blue satin bedspread, and Marion buried her face in the cool petals.

"They are beautiful, Harro," she said affectionately. "You must let Judith see the blooming fields of the Betuwe. She is inside way too much, the poor dear."

Harro turned his head toward Judith and searched for her eyes, as though to see what she thought of the proposal.

Her glance took in his blond head and she knew only one thing at this moment: how terribly much she loved him.

"Can you live without Judith for a day?" she heard Harro ask.

"I have Inge home, too," Marion replied. "I have no lack of helping hands, Son."

He kissed his mother good-bye, and on the way out he grazed Judith's cheek as well. "Tomorrow," he said. "Mother's word is law."

That evening he brought it up again. "Do I bore you?" he asked bluntly.

"Never," she promptly reacted. "Where did you get that idea?"

"Because Mother thought it necessary to give me a hint. I don't take you out enough."

She had never had such a wonderful winter and decided not to take his question seriously. "That's true," she said, "you have locked me up in your castle from day one and hardly given me the chance to see other people. You want to keep me completely to yourself, tyrant!"

"I thought so." He kidded her, but her tone had half convinced him.

She nodded good-naturedly over her magazine.

"When I am tired of looking at your face, I will let you know," she promised. She blew him a kiss. "But for the time being there is not much chance of that."

She buried herself again in the article she was reading, but Harro was not quite finished with her. He stuck out one of his long legs and, with the tip of his toes, pulled the magazine out of her hands.

"I still don't know if you want to go out with me tomorrow," he stated.

She lifted her face toward him. "Of course I want to. With pleasure. But not because I feel deprived. Your mother probably feels bad that I am spending so much of my time with her. But that is nonsense. It is a joy to be with her, not a sacrifice."

The next day the weather again put its best foot forward. The fields of the Betuwe, with its meadows and lakes, its white orchards and its village churches, was beautiful sleeping against the dikes.

Early in the afternoon they crossed the Rhine on the ferry to Wageningen. The Rhine was like a glistening highway through the flood plains, flanked by chimneys of the brick factories along the bank.

"Now we are coming to holy ground," Harro warned.

Judith was not familiar with Wageningen. "Is it an interesting city?"

"Not really," he said frankly, "but I love it. I have so many pleasant memories of this city that one afternoon is far too short to let you share them all."

They parked the car at the foot of Wageningen hill, which rose suddenly from the plain like a natural fort.

They walked through the experimental gardens of the Agricultural College, filled with blooming hedges, and over the narrow paths along the ridge of the hill which offered a breathtaking panorama of the river below at every turn.

A tugboat slowly made its way down the river, and a lone sailor tried to tack every breath of wind.

Harro told her of the many hours he spent on the river as a member of the student sculling team, and of the competitions he took part in at that time.

Later they sat down on a bench to watch the miniature cows down in the valley.

"How many girls have you walked with here?" Judith wanted to know.

He looked at her from the corner of his eye. "Should I have kept track?" he teased.

She returned his amused glance. "No," she said, playing along. "It is none of my business, anyway. But I get envious just thinking about it," she candidly added.

"Then you still have a lot to learn," Harro confirmed like a father.

He could with a jest bring up the most profound subjects, and this time Judith understood with a jolt that she had no idea how difficult it was for him to never make jealous comments or ask questions about her previous life, even though he was completely in the dark as far as her past was concerned.

Soon they descended the hill again. Judith took off her sweater along the way. "It is warm," she sighed. "It would be nice to go sit down by the Rhine for a while, don't you think?"

"Let's go," he agreed.

They left the car parked where it was and walked the short distance back to the ferry, where a rough, narrow path traveled right along the river and led to the breakwaters that extended several yards out into the water. By a rugged stand of alders they lay down.

The cattails had already blossomed; only a few solitary fluffy balls were still to be seen.

Harro had stretched out to full length in the grass. He reached a lazy arm toward her. "Come to me."

"There may be some guy fishing on the other side of these trees," Judith warily suggested.

"Of course there isn't. Come on."

It was very quiet around them.

The insects buzzed in the orchard behind them, and in the distance they could hear the rusty groan of a ferry pulling into its moorings and the sound of a truck making its way off the boat.

When even those sounds faded away, the silence was complete.

Judith removed her sunglasses. She lay with her face turned toward the sun, eyes closed, her head nestled against Harro's chest. She felt his warm, trusted hand encircling her arm.

"If you could make a wish, what would you wish for?" he asked after a while.

She held her breath for a moment. "I don't know," she lied. "I have nothing left to wish for. How about you?"

"Maybe a little boy," he said dreamily, "or a daughter called Marion, just like Mother. But she must have your eyes and your elegance."

His tender words were like barbs ripping open her soul. But it was a familiar pain for her. In the five months that had passed since their wedding, they had gone through several situations like this one.

In the early days of their marriage, Harro had asked her in one of their most intimate moments whether she would think it terrible if they were to have a baby soon.

His mouth was soft against her skin. She was tired and full

of love and did not have the strength to put a damper on one of the most glorious moments in both their lives.

"I think it would be wonderful," she had whispered.

It was not a lie: She would have thought it wonderful. But it would never be realized, and so she had remained with the feeling that at that very moment she had begun to deceive him.

After this first equivocation, the second could not be far behind. She had walked a wide, careful loop around the feared subject, but the few times that Harro brought it up again, she could not bear to tell him.

She was able to avoid outright lies, and when her cowardice accused her, she was able to fool herself into thinking that it was so innocent just to dream along with his sweet little dream for a little while—a dream that had always been her own.

"What would you prefer, a boy or a girl?" Harro continued, unaware of the pain he was causing her.

"It wouldn't matter to me," Judith said passionately. "Not at all. If only it was warm and alive and part of me. If only I could see you in it."

If her ardor seemed strange to him, he did not let on.

He softly stroked her arm while his quiet voice carried on, close to her ear. "It was nearly sixty years ago that the last child was born at the House of Herewaarden. It is no longer equipped for children, but we could pick out a room on the sunny side and set up a room with all the cute little things that you can get today."

"Doll curtains," she confessed with yearning. "And some of those precious little stuffed animals."

"There must be an antique cradle somewhere," Harro said, "but that is probably no good, is it? In these modern times. Do you think my kids will get used to me?"

"Oh, no," she mused. "You will be the ideal father. You will teach them so many things before they even realize that they arc actually learning. You will make sure that every party is truly a party, but you will be strong and resolute when it appears necessary."

"Do you really think so?"

"Oh, yes."

"Why?"

"Because you have the patience of Uncle Diederick, the *joie de vivre* of your mother, and the authority of your father. That's why."

"Wait a minute," he interrupted, bemused. "Don't I have any faults?"

"If you do," she said with a glimmer of sarcasm, "then you are very good at disguising them."

Harro laughed.

"What a disappointment it will be for you if today or tomorrow my true nature comes to the surface," he joked.

Their conversation continued down the same lighthearted path for the time being, but that evening Harro returned to the subject without warning—more urgently this time, without joking.

They sat across from each other in the restaurant they chose for supper. After the final course they sat to enjoy a cup of coffee.

A small hurricane lamp threw subdued light over their hands, and the falling darkness underscored the intimacy of their togetherness.

Silence had fallen between them, and Judith sensed that Harro was observing her.

"You must have watched me closely," he suddenly said, summing up his thoughts, "if you can tell me so precisely where I derived my characteristics."

"It was not such a difficult task, getting to know you," she answered. "You have been an open book for me from the very first day."

It was not meant to be derogatory, but to Harro's heightened sensitivity her words contained a hint of mockery that immediately occasioned a cooling in the way he was taking in her visage.

"I must admit that where that is concerned I am at a distinct disadvantage," he said with a note of bitterness. "Sometimes I get the feeling that I am always approaching you but never quite arriving."

He saw the consternation rise in her eyes, and it made her attempt at humor all the more pathetic. "I have given myself to you kit and caboodle. What more can I do?"

"Kit and caboodle—yes," he affirmed, "but not heart and soul. I am wandering through a house where I am free to peruse, where I am free to come and go and am welcome. But there is one room that is locked, where the blinds are drawn."

Her eyes still read consternation and confusion. She bit her lip.

Harro let her be for a few moments, but when she maintained her silence, he apologized as he had the week before. "I know that I have no right to talk. I am the one who locked that room."

"Are you sorry?" she asked with difficulty.

He nodded. "Yes. But not for myself. For you. It would have been better for you to have made a clean start. I did not see it at the time. I'm sorry."

She wondered whether he was waiting for her to speak. He probably was. But she couldn't. Not yet.

Her heart screamed when she thought of his tender words of that afternoon about a daughter called Marion.

"You have chosen a very unfortunate place to discuss this subject," she said sharply. "I do not want to discuss it any further here, Harro."

He made a concessive gesture. "You said that I had the

proverbial patience of Uncle Diederick. I hope I can live up to it, Judith."

He stood up and helped her with her coat, apparently considering the discussion closed.

"Would you like to drive home?" he offered, as though nothing had happened.

"Please," she eagerly accepted, thankful for the respite he was granting her.

For the first time it was keenly impressed on her mind how far she had plunged herself into misery by burying her head in the sand. She would need time to seriously consider how she could make her conduct acceptable to Harro.

The thought of that conversation, which now appeared inevitable, weighed heavy on her heart.

❧ Chapter 16 ❧

It was custom that Harro and Judith spend at least one evening a week at the Warbler.

Even if it were only for a little while, Marion tried to be downstairs when they came.

Rein and Paula were also often part of the group, but recently they had taken it upon themselves to try to spread out their visits somewhat. Marion grew continually weaker, and since it was not in her nature to spare herself, the others had to do their utmost to conserve her dwindling energy.

This time Judith and Harro were relatively early.

Lucy came and greeted them in the hall. "Mother is still upstairs," she said.

Harro ascended the stairs three at a time. In his mother's room he found not only his parents, but also Inge, who was helping Marion put on her bathrobe.

"Shall I carry you downstairs, Mother?" he offered.

"Don't even try it," Reinier said dryly. "You have your own wife. I'll carry mine."

Harro and Inge exchanged a quick glance.

As long as it is possible. They completed their father's unfinished thought in their minds.

Marion laughed at them. "You just go ahead," she said. "We will come in a minute."

When her mother was in place on the daybed in the sitting room, Lucy went for the coffee.

"Did you finish your homework, little gnome?" Reinier asked, with a yank at Lucy's blond braid.

"No," she said defiantly, "and I could care less. I'm flunking anyway."

Everyone understood why she had not been able to keep her mind on her studies, and no one held it against her. But it would be a shame if she were to actually fail.

"Maybe it will get better," Harro consoled. "When are finals?"

"June tenth."

"Would you like me to help you with your work these last five or six weeks?" he offered.

Her gray eyes lit up.

"Oh would you?" she gushed, and as an aside said to Judith, "You would be surprised at how clearly Harro can explain things."

"I would believe it in a minute, Lucy," Judith replied, with something of the dry humor that was the predominant tone of the conversations in this house. "He made something very clear to me once. Know what I mean?"

They all laughed.

Judith couldn't help but think of Harro's statement on the evening he told her for the first time about Mother's sickness: "Until you have met some of my housemates, I can't rightly describe the atmosphere around the house, but *subdued* is in any case not the right word."

Now she knew.

She looked at the striking face of her father-in-law and felt a certain kinship with him. He did not take his eyes off his wife for a moment. He was consciously counting the hours of bittersweet happiness that had been given to him—just as she was.

Her subconscious warned her of the catastrophe hanging over her head when she divulged her trickery. The longer it went on, the more acutely she recognized the mistake she had made. She had consciously left Harro with the impression that the secret in her life was an old love affair that he could decently push to one side as "the past."

But she had no right to hide behind that generous gesture of his, because she knew full well that her former grief had left consequences for the present and the future in its wake. That she had remained silent with all the consequences it entailed had been a capital blunder on her part. One for which she would someday have to pay with the loss of his respect, perhaps even his love.

He could forgive her for everything except the fact that she withheld from him the confidence he had made the only condition when he asked her to marry him.

Harro had not yet returned to their conversation in the restaurant. He was apparently leaving it to her.

She prayed every night in desperation for the courage she needed, but it was as though she were banging on a closed door.

She hardly dared to expect that God would listen to her, in light of the fact that she only served Him in order to please Harro. In spite of her regular church attendance of the last few months, the only real relation that existed between God and herself was the breathtaking jealousy that sometimes fell over her when she recognized the power and courage others seemed to derive from their faith—especially Marion.

While her thoughts piled one on top of the other, the conversation had gone on. It had passed her by completely, and her attention was not recalled until her mother-in-law finished a comment with the words, ". . . and who can allow the luxury of having two kind licensed nurses at their disposal?"

"Not to mention the fact that Inge can without any objection present herself as a half doctor," Reinier added, teasing. "She even operates when she gets the chance. Did you know that, Judith?"

Inge put a finger to her lips. "Without authorization, so don't tell a soul, please."

Her voice was hoarse and more or less subdued. There was something the matter with her vocal chords that caused the hoarseness from which she would never entirely recover.

Judith's curiosity had been piqued. She looked quizzically at her sister-in-law.

"Yes, it is true," she confirmed. "It is a running joke with Jaques and Marie-Louise that their father and mother know each other from the inside out. Five years ago Bram had to operate on my gallbladder, and I had to operate on his appendix three years later."

She related it without fanfare, and Judith began, baffled, "But how . . . ?"

"Oh, it was not as simple as it seems in retrospect," Inge honestly admitted. "I died a thousand deaths from worry.

"It was an acute case of appendicitis: a routine operation that I had observed enough times to know precisely how it had to be done. But the fact that it was Bram made it all different.

"It all started very early in the morning. Bram had not slept for hours because of the pain. When he woke me up, he knew precisely what the problem was and had figured out in detail what we would have to do.

"Under any other circumstances, it would have been cause for panic. Transportation to the nearest hospital was out of the question because of the time it required, and calling a surgeon presented exactly the same problem. Postponing an operation would at the very least lead to peritonitis.

"The only alternative was to do the operation myself, and I had to come to grips with that fact on an empty stomach. It was not easy for Bram to entrust another with such a difficult task, but when there is no choice, he can be as hard as nails.

"I didn't know what to do, and kept whispering, 'I don't dare, Bram. I don't dare.'

" 'Think of William's leg,' he said with grim humor. That was his way of giving my confidence a boost. William's leg was my first act of valor. He was a native fisherman, a great guy. William had had a run-in with a jaguar, and it happened near our settlement when Bram was away for a week on an emergency run to a native village in the area.

"The leg had to be amputated immediately. I had to make the decision, and I had to make sure I did it right, too. With the help of two Creole brothers, I did manage to pull it off, and it all turned out all right. Bram was beside himself with pride when he heard the whole account upon his return.

"William has had a wooden leg for years now, and gets around like an old pro, but now he won't leave the immediate vicinity of the hospital. His leg has become something of a proverb in our house.

"But to put it simply, at that critical moment, William's leg appeared to fall short of bringing my morale up to par.

"I had to do many other things over the course of the years that were actually beyond my capabilities, but that was with strangers, and I was able to keep a cool head without any difficulty.

"But this was Bram, the central point of my life; and not only mine. You can hardly imagine the dominant position he holds in our community there. He is not only the doctor; they ask his advice on everything. He serves as judge, architect, agricultural consultant. The entire project that we had over the years struggled with God's help to establish stood or fell with his health. That thought paralyzed me.

"Bram did not give me much time to adjust to the idea. When I had dressed, he said, biting off the pain he was feeling, 'Get everything prepared for the operation, and call Samuel. We will have to hold a powwow.'

"Samuel was the Creole evangelist in the settlement. In those days he lived with us. He was a very kind young man. Harro knows him. I don't know what those two talked about while I was giving orders in the hospital, still trembling right down to my toes.

"When I returned, Samuel took me firmly by the arm. 'Mrs. Dubois,' he commanded, 'you must do what the doctor says, but you are not alone. I will make sure that all who have a voice and can fold their hands are in the chapel in a half hour. As long as you are working, we will pray God for wisdom and confidence for you.'

"I will always remember that moment as one of the most gripping moments of my entire life."

Inge fell silent and lowered her head, carried back to the distant green world where she had more than once incomprehensibly experienced God's presence.

"And how did it turn out?" Judith asked, fascinated.

Inge raised her face once again. The lines that life had etched there spoke their own language. "Very well," she said quietly. "I did what I had to do in the confidence that God held my hand. And He did.

"A little less than a week later, Bram was walking around

again, and Samuel held a special service of thanks that Sunday.

"Such moments form a counterbalance to the unmentionable number of sorrows, frustrations, stench, and struggles—the ingredients that seem to make up eighty percent of life in the jungle. At such moments you feel in your very marrow that our lives indeed have meaning and that we are all part of the comprehensive plan of God."

Judith spent the entire evening under the sway of Inge's story, which was really nothing less than a testimony.

As they walked along the dark path back to the House of Herewaarden, Harro said, "You asked last week where Inge and Bram get the strength and courage to continue rowing against the current. I think this evening you received a sufficient response to your question."

"Yes," she said with a sigh. "It must be wonderful to have so many people praying for you when you face the most difficult task of your life."

He agreed and returned to the day's affairs, but her words had been chiseled into his memory.

Several days later he was still puzzling over the question of whether there was much more behind her sighs than she was letting on.

❧ Chapter 17 ❧

Now that Inge was in the Netherlands, she wanted to take advantage of the opportunity to see her in-laws.

Bram's parents had died, but three of his brothers and his only sister, Marlies, were easy enough to find.

Soon after her return to Borg, she spent an entire day with Marlies, who had always been her best friend and was married to Arend van der Mast, a former fellow student of Inge's. Arend had a doctor's practice in a village not far from Borg, and Reinier himself brought Inge and picked her up again.

But when after a week she expressed a desire to go to Boskoop, where Gert Dubois owned a tree nursery, Judith offered, "If Harro can do without the car for a day, I will take you to Boskoop. While you are with your brother- and sister-in-law, I can go visit my mother in Wassenaar."

Inge gladly accepted her offer.

When Harro had given his consent, she called Boskoop to announce her arrival.

On the agreed-upon day, they left in the morning after their usual duties at the Warbler.

"What do you think about Mother?" Judith asked, once they were in the car.

"Another few weeks—at the most," Inge said concisely. "It could be days, in fact. Actually I am not very happy to be so far from her today," she added, "but I long to see the faces of my other loved ones after all these years. And my time is precious, Judith. I don't want to stay too long from the mission post. My heart is yearning for Bram and the children."

She smiled briefly at her long summary. "My heart is being pulled in all directions," she said. "Do you know that feeling?"

Judith gave neither a yes nor no. "Be happy for that," she reacted rather harshly. "You are more fortunate than some."

A long silence ensued.

It was busy on the road, and Inge—remembering the numerous warnings Harro had sent along with them—did not want to distract her sister-in-law from her driving. She had only had her driver's license for a short time.

Inge, too, had driven once in a blue moon before. But in the twelve years of her absence, the traffic had become so much more intense that she would not have dared to get behind the wheel again. The noises of the jungle that had once frightened her had become more pleasant to her than the roar of engines.

It was Judith who resumed the conversation.

"How old were you when you lost your mother?" she asked.

"Five years old. But I hardly knew her. She had been sick for a long time before she died."

"And did you ever have the feeling that you were a step-child?"

"Oh, yes," Inge said. "Unfairly, but I did."

Judith, who was expecting a denial in light of the wholesome atmosphere in the Warbler, looked askance at her.

"Really? You form such a perfect family that I can hardly imagine there was ever any dissonance."

Inge had to laugh. "Put that out of your mind," she said. "We were certainly no saints—not one of us. But I know what you mean. You have only known us since Mother's illness, and that has intensified, so to speak, all our feelings of love and togetherness. I get the impression that we are all consciously trying to make these last few months as happy as possible for her."

"That's true," Judith affirmed. "And you are right; such a common effort automatically strengthens the bonds among you."

"There has always been a harmonious atmosphere at home," Inge thought out loud, "but not to this degree. And don't forget that the most difficult personalities are not here. If you only knew how Rein and Charlotte used to fight, you couldn't describe it with a book. Did you meet Charlotte yet?"

"A couple of times," Judith said. "She is a beauty."

"That could very well be," Inge replied. "She was always a pretty child. But I have never seen her as an adult. She does have a very difficult personality, though, Judith. Hold on especially to her when Mother is gone. Harro has always had a lot of influence with her. As far as Rein is concerned, he is a fine man, but as a child he could become disturbingly angry, just like Father."

"Your father? Angry?"

"Count on it. My earliest memories of Mother are from when she was still *Miss Marion* to me. More than once I broke down in tears at the way Father snapped at her.

"That was when Mama still was dying, and he certainly must not have had it easy at that time. But I remember that we kids always had respect for his temper. And Mother also has her faults. Trust me."

"You are robbing me of an illusion," Judith said.

Inge shook her head. "That is not my intention. I am only trying to make you understand that people do not have to be perfect in order to be loved, and that faults and shortcomings do not have to be an obstacle to a happy marriage."

"And why do you feel it necessary to bring that so emphatically to my attention?" she asked somewhat rigidly.

"Because you are bending over backwards to please Harro," Inge said honestly. "You are doing your utmost to be the perfect woman for him, but who says he wants a perfect woman?"

"You just arrived here," Judith answered sharply, "and I can't believe that you are clairvoyant. Has Harro been talking to you about me?"

Inge looked at her indignantly. "Of course not," she said curtly. "Harro would never do that, and you know that very well."

Judith raised her hackles. "Oh, no," she said spitefully. "Rein has a bad temper, and Charlotte is a pain, but Harro can do no wrong. Harro is everyone's darling. For Harro the best is never good enough."

Inge's indignation changed to astonishment. Sure, everyone loved Harro—that had always been the case. But anyone could see that Judith outdid everyone on that score. Her unreasonable outburst proved beyond a shadow of a doubt that Marion had been right: Judith was walking around with something stuck in her craw.

She ignored her sister-in-law's emotion and said, "I'll be frank with you. It was Mother who spoke to me about you two. She has really begun to love you these last few months, Judith."

Judith shored up her defenses when she felt the vulnerability that this comment created in her. "No need to beat around the bush or sweeten the pill," she sternly rebuked.

"Whoever thinks I am not good enough for Harro can just say it!"

Inge laid her slender brown hand on Judith's sleeve. "Only one person thinks that," she said gently, "and that person is you. Apparently without any reason."

"Oh, yes, there is a reason," Judith said.

She looked straight ahead, intent on the road before her. Then she said with sullen, choppy words, "I cannot have children."

"No!" Inge reacted in shock. "Are you serious?" Her thoughts were tumbling toward Bram and the wonder of a newborn baby that he had four times laid in her arms.

"Do I look like I am joking?" Judith asked wryly.

"No, of course not. But I was so shocked. How long have you known?"

Judith did not have to calculate long in order to answer her question. "Five years and seven months," she said. That terrible spring in which her world caved in around her could never be erased from her memory.

Inge, who had expected a completely different answer, looked at her, not understanding. "But you and Harro . . . ," she began.

"It is a long story," she warned her, "and not very happy, I'm afraid."

"Do you want to talk about it?"

"No," Judith admitted, "but if I do not talk to someone, I am going to choke on it someday."

❧ Chapter 18 ❧

Inge took note of her sister-in-law's consternation with an attentive look.

They rode through the green landscape of South Holland, with its canals and windmills and countless poplars on the horizon.

"Let's stop for a while," Inge suggested.

"But you have to get to your family in Boskoop," Judith objected.

"I have not seen them in twelve years. A half hour one way or the other will not make any difference."

"All right, then," Judith agreed, driving the small car onto a side road. "You're right not to trust my presence of mind at this moment and to want to preserve your life."

"And yours," Inge added quietly, without taking offense at Judith's cynical tone.

Then Judith told her everything about Jan Willem, about the doctor's tests, about the verdict of the specialist, about the brokcn engagement. It sounded infinitely emotionless and weary, as though she had told it countless times before.

She told about her departure abroad to Pakistan, that was a flight; about her stay in Pakistan, Persia, and Alaska, very summarily, because in retrospect she had the feeling that she had been barely alive at that time.

But when she began to talk about Constantine, more animation was apparent in her voice.

"There I met Harro," she said. "Three weeks before I left for the Netherlands. He was immediately head over heels in love with me. Why, I still don't know.

"But I underestimated him. I found him a boy, too idealistic, too green for the merciless world in which we have to live. I had some fun with his adoration, but I intended to stay out of range.

"But even before the three weeks were up, I realized how wrong I had been about him and that I would not be able to escape his charms as easily as I had imagined.

"I was becoming more attached to him by the day, and when I realized that, I knew I would have to disappear from his life. After all, if he were to ask me to marry him, I would have to tell him what was wrong with me, and then there were two possibilities: He could send me away, as Jan Willem had, and I could not bear that thought; or he could accept the disappointment for my sake and automatically throw away his opportunity to have a happy family like the one in which he grew up. And I could no more bear that thought.

"That is why I left Constantine twenty-four hours earlier than expected without leaving an address—in the hope that we would be able to forget about each other."

"But it did not work."

"Not very well. But at least I was at peace then. I had acted honorably and honestly."

"And you had. And then?"

"Then Harro came back from Algeria, and the first thing he did was track down my address. He looked me up in Nijmegen, where I had found work, and everything started all over again.

"I was facing the same dilemma.

"Harro had in the meantime sensed that something awful had happened in my life that I was still suffering from, but he was too courteous to ask direct questions, and I could not bring myself to speak the bitter truth.

"I knew well enough by then that he would not leave me in the lurch, but I feared the moment when the uninhibited spontaneity that attracted me to him would become an obligatory faithfulness."

She fell silent until Inge broke the silence with the words, "I fully understand how difficult it was for you. Was it a long time before you were able to muster the courage?"

Judith looked at Inge. "You still don't understand what I am getting at?" she asked. "Then I'll tell you in so many words: I have gotten just as far as I was six months ago."

"Judith!" Inge called, taken aback. "You mean to tell me that Harro doesn't know that you cannot have children? After all these months?"

Judith nodded mutely.

She leaned her arms against the steering wheel, laid her head on her arms, and cried. "I did not want to deceive him, Inge," she sobbed. "Really, I didn't." In fits and starts, the whole story came out. How she had tried before to inform Harro, and that decisive moment on the viewing tower. How he had obstructed her with his generous point of view that the past was past and he desired no further disclosures from her. How she had weakened at that moment, thinking it would be kinder and more humane to allow him his dreams.

"I understand it so far," Inge resumed, "but since you have been married, you must have had innumerable opportunities to recognize the mistake you made and correct it. I am married, too, so I know what I am talking about, and I assume that you must have soon realized that silence without lies is impossible. Because if you are happy, you talk about these things. You have dreams, plans . . ."

"Not I," Judith said sadly.

"But Harro certainly did?" Inge delved.

Judith nodded. "Yes, of course. It went so treacherously unnoticed." She spoke very quietly, looking straight ahead. "Once I had yielded to the temptation to talk along with him, the second time went easier, and the third, and the fourth. I love him so terribly much, Inge," she confessed with restrained passion. "And when he says things—as he did last week about a little daughter who would have to be named *Marion* just like Mother, but should have my eyes—then I become weak inside and simply cannot shatter his dream. I want to shield his happiness with both hands, rather than cause him grief."

Inge immediately knew how to lay her finger on the wound.

"But Harro is no child anymore!" she said. "He is a full-grown man; he is your husband! Do you really think he would appreciate your protecting his happy-go-lucky nature at the cost of your own peace of mind? You have carried your cross alone this entire winter—a cross you should have shared. You have deprived Harro of his right to comfort and help you, and I fear that he will be most offended by that."

Judith nervously bit her lip. "So you think I should tell him?"

"No matter what. You can't build your happiness on a lie. Just imagine what will happen if you continue to bury your head in the sand. You have only been married five months, but if you don't eventually get pregnant, you will have to submit to a doctor's examination. You will get the same verdict you got before, and then what? Then Harro will know;

then you will be released from the task of having to tell him. But do you really think that you will be able to keep quiet forever? You are not unscrupulous enough for that, my friend. Besides, what basis would remain for your marriage? Love demands trust."

Judith began to cry again. "I know that I am a coward, but I don't dare bring it up. I just don't dare. He will be so disappointed in me. And if he stopped loving me, I would rather die."

"Love does not allow itself to be killed off that easily," Inge assured her. "You must swallow the bitter pill as soon as possible, girl. That is the best solution."

Judith nodded wordlessly. A deep, heartfelt sigh escaped her. Then she got control of herself. She dried her tears and with mechanical movements began to straighten herself up.

Inge felt sorry for her. *How you have gotten yourself all entangled for no reason,* she thought. *I would not want to be in your shoes.*

Slowly she began to realize that Judith had arranged this combined trip to Boskoop with the full intention of confessing.

"Why did you pick me to talk to?" she wanted to know.

Judith lowered her pocket comb. "Because I was broken up by that story you told this week, and especially by the way God was with you at the time."

"God is here too, Judith."

"But your faith is so amazingly practical. You have no time for theological hairsplitting. You don't theorize; you simply bow your heads in situations of need. You stick the knife in and blindly trust God to help. I would give anything to have that kind of trust, Inge."

The words were strangely familiar to Inge. It was the same distress call she had sent out to Bram years before, when a violent struggle was tearing her life apart.

She wondered whether her sister-in-law would find it helpful if she were to relate some of the things that happened back then.

Judith had in the meantime regained her composure. She returned the car to the highway and they silently continued their journey. After a while, Inge asked, "How do you think I viewed life in the jungle when I was twenty-three years old?"

"Very unpleasant," Judith assumed, startled.

"Unpleasant? I *hated* the idea of going there, because I was scared to death. Afraid of snakes and crocodiles and sharks; afraid of the native superstitions; afraid of loneliness and the heat. You just said twice in a row, 'I don't dare.' I said the same thing to myself a thousand times over in those days. I wanted so desperately to be strong and undaunted, because I loved Bram, and that love pulled my heart, but the security of home pulled just as hard, and I could not take the decisive step. The struggle lasted for months, and toward the end there was little left except bitterness."

Judith's interest had been awakened. "And then?" she prodded.

"Then I met someone who showed me a way out of the labyrinth of doubt. We had only a brief conversation, but a couple of days later he sent me something that he carried with him for many years in his wallet. It was a New Year's card in English that influenced my life and that of Bram in a very substantial way."

"What did it say?"

Inge had long since memorized the words, which she quoted in Dutch.

I said to the man who stood at the gate of the year:
"Give me a light, that I may tread safely into the known."

And he replied: "Go out into the darkness and put your hand into the hand of God. That shall be to thee better than a light and safer than a known way."

"That hit the nail on the head," Judith noted.

She was fully aware of the fact that Inge was not telling this story because she wanted to kill the time, and so she continued. "I know that was the word that set you free, but do you really see any similarities?"

"Certainly I see similarities," Inge resumed. "Why do you always say, 'I don't dare'? Why do you lack courage? It is because you don't know how Harro will react to the fact that you have kept him away from your deepest need. The fact that you don't know has become an obsession with you. You imagine the most terrible things, and that is why your fear of saying anything grows the longer you wait. But once you believe that God has brought you together, that He would not allow His blessing to be spoken over your marriage with the intention of having you separate in a half year after a fierce fight, then you are well on the right path. You have already realized that you made mistakes and it is your moral duty to set things right. Then you can count on God's help when you take that leap into the dark, as I did when I had to perform that unexpected operation. It may be that Harro will become very angry. He is a human, after all, and let's be honest, you do deserve it a bit, even though there have been mitigating circumstances. But he cannot become so angry that his love will not win in the end!"

"Do you think so?"

"You must know my brother," Inge said, full of pride.

She suddenly laughed openly and disarmingly, and Judith answered her laugh in spite of herself.

"You have helped me immensely," she said gratefully.

❧ Chapter 19 ❧

That evening they returned to Borg.

The Warbler was emitting light from every side when they drove up; even the antique lamp next to the door was shining.

The first thing they noticed was Erik's large motorcycle that was haphazardly parked on the garden path, as though its rider had entered the house with in haste.

"Erik is home," Inge said.

Judith nodded. She sensed the uneasiness in her words, but she had no time to comment further. Another car drove up behind them.

They clambered out to greet Rein.

"Good thing you are back," he said quickly. "Mother is not good at all."

"What happened?" Inge asked.

"She had a serious hemorrhage in the afternoon. The doctor has been here for hours. He is afraid she will not last much longer."

"But why didn't you call us? We would have returned earlier!"

"Harro would not permit it. He did not want to run the risk of having you get into an accident."

Judith stood by dejectedly. It had not sunk in completely. "An accident? Why?" she asked, dazed.

"Because you would have rushed if you had known," Rein explained. "Do you think you would not have been nervous? You have not had that much experience yet. Come on."

He took them both by the arm and the three of them walked together up the gravel garden path to the front door. Rein had the key.

As soon as they were in the hall, Harro poked his head out of a room. His eyes lit up when he saw them. They walked quickly toward each other and Harro threw a long arm around Judith. "Thank God I have you back in one piece," he said softly.

Judith lifted her face toward him. "Is your mother dying?" she asked tensely.

He nodded silently, and her eyes filled with tears.

"The doctor wanted to have her taken to Dintelborg for a final blood transfusion," Harro explained, "but Father refused. It made no sense to prolong it any further. She would rather die in the Warbler today than in the hospital tomorrow."

They went into the sitting room where Lucy and Erik sought comfort from each other and Rein and Inge stood talking in front of the window.

Judith greeted her youngest brother-in-law.

"How long have you been home, Erik?" she asked.

"An hour. I left Rotterdam as soon as Rein called me."

"Charlotte is on her way," Lucy shared. "She will be arriving at Schipol tonight. Aunt Edith will pick her up there, and then they will come here."

139

"Aunt Edith is Mother's only sister," Harro explained as an aside. "She lives in The Hague."

Judith nodded her understanding. "The beauty specialist," she said. "I met her at our wedding. Where is Paula?" she asked.

"She is in my room," Lucy said. "Rein sent her upstairs to rest for a few hours. She did not feel very good." She stood up to make coffee.

When Lucy had left the room, Harro said generally, "She keeps her chin up, doesn't she?"

"All too well," Inge added. She could not get over the fact that the little doll with the blond curls called Lucy could have grown up since she had been away. Now she was a full-grown woman who perfectly resembled old pictures of Marion.

After a few minutes, Lucy came back with the coffee. "Would you like something to eat?" she asked.

Judith shook her head emphatically no.

They sat silently together; only now and again did a word break the silence. After a while, Paula rejoined them. She was very pale, but so was everyone else.

They all wanted to go upstairs, but something was holding them back—a deferential reluctance that prevented them from disturbing their parents' final moments together.

Then the door opened and Reinier stood on the threshold. The lines in his face appeared deeper than ever. He took them all in with a long, painful look.

"Children . . . ," he said.

No one dared ask him anything.

It was Lucy who broke the silence. She stood up and placed her cheek against that of her father. Large tears slowly made their way down her face. "Say it," she sniffled.

"Don't cry, my little adjutant," he said tenderly, as though they were alone. "Mother wants to see you—you and the other children. Come." He laid his arm around her slender shoulders and took her upstairs to Marion's room.

One by one they said good-bye, almost without words, since Marion was too weak to speak.

Charlotte, who had just arrived, remained inside the longest. None of the others begrudged her this.

The regular contact they had had with their mother during the long winter while Charlotte was in Rome had been a continual good-bye. All of them had, in their own way, experienced the cheerful power of faith radiating from her as a blessing to their souls.

Charlotte had missed more than she was able to regain.

The doctor had withdrawn. There was nothing more he could do for his patient, and he had the strong feeling that he was superfluous here.

Evening turned to night, but no one considered going to bed.

Not a sound came from upstairs.

When the clock struck two, Rein said hoarsely, "Someone should go check. Father can't be doing very well. He has had such a long period of stress."

They looked at one another. Each of them recalled what Reinier had said when he finally brought the crying Charlotte downstairs. The edge on his voice and the expression of unspeakable grief in his eyes would not be easy to forget.

"Let me be alone with her now," he had said.

Although they were all adults, their father's words still bore the same authority they always had.

Nevertheless, they knew that Rein was right.

When no one objected to his comment, he took the initiative.

"Inge," he said, with a quick nod of his head, "you have more authority than we do, under the circumstances."

She understood and willingly stood up.

For a moment it appeared as though Lucy might protest, but she fell back in silent weakness.

Inge walked up the stairs and knocked softly on the door of the sickroom. When there was no response, she entered.

She saw immediately that Marion had died.

Her father sat motionless next to the bed.

When she put her arms around his shoulders, he appeared to awaken from a daze. "I couldn't leave her alone," he said, as though he had to defend himself against an unspoken accusation. When he stood up, he tottered, as though bearing a load that was too heavy for him.

Inge had to support him, and her heart overflowed for his sake. Never in her life had she seen her father so unsettled.

"Come," she said quietly. "You must rest for a while. You have demanded too much of yourself."

He looked at her as though he was for the first time conscious of who it was beside him. "Inge." He struggled. "What were we alone, you and I, before she was there to make us happy? And now she is gone."

He laid his brown, muscular hand on Marion's white forehead. "More than thirty years," he said to himself. "More than thirty years, and it was but a breath, a wrinkle in time. All my todays have become yesterdays, Inge. My today has become a yesterday."

"No," said Inge firmly. "No, Father. Today is always tomorrow. Mother knew that, too, and you will remember it in the morning."

She managed to get him to his own room, and he promised that he would lie down.

When she returned to the others, Lucy fell apart, her eyes wild. "Mother is dead!" she cried with a catch in her voice.

"Yes," Inge confirmed. "Mother is dead."

Unconsciously they all stood up.

Lucy passed them by, but Inge took her by the arm.

"What are you going to do?"

"I want to go to Father!"

Inge shook her head. "Father is exhausted," she said. "He can't take any more, Lucy. He must sleep."

"Let me go!" she said, angry and jealous. "You had no right to be there. She wasn't even your mother!"

"She was the best friend I ever had," Inge said, gently.

She did her best not to feel hurt. Lucy was just a child, almost twenty years younger than she; she was consumed by grief and stress. She thought of the defeated man upstairs who so desperately needed his rest, and did not know what to do.

"Harro?" she said indecisively, intuitively calling in his help.

"Let her go," he said without hesitation. "Those two need each other."

❧ Chapter 20 ❧

Strange, confused days followed.

Harro arranged practically all the details for the funeral, and as a result was often away from home. It made Judith nervous and agitated.

The long conversation with Inge had given her courage. When they had returned from Boskoop, she had the sincere intention of talking with Harro that evening. But now that all the developments surrounding the death of Marion had intervened, she had not been able to carry out her intention.

The longer the delay lasted, the more she felt her inner resolve ebb away, and it was almost with a sense of panic that she looked for an occasion to speak privately with Harro before all her courage melted away.

But she had little opportunity to see him.

When he was not away, he was on the telephone, and when he was finally free, he was commandeered by Charlotte or Lucy.

When they finally went to bed, he was dead tired from all the worries and grief for his mother, for which he had no time during the day.

She did not want to take the chance of bringing him more problems.

For three days she swallowed her vexation and restlessness, but when he announced once again that he had to be away that evening, the measure was full, and she angrily fell on him. "Why must you do everything yourself? Can't Rein do something for once?"

Harro looked at her, rather puzzled. "Will you consider the fact that Rein has to run the factory alone now that Father is not there?" he asked coolly, "and that it is much easier for me to break away from my work than it is for him?"

"Does he stay at the factory all night, too?" she asked sarcastically.

"I don't know. But I imagine he is happy when he can go home. Paula has not been well for days now. Now that we are on the subject, I thought you could maybe take the two little ones for a day this week. Then Paula can get back on track a little after all this emotional upheaval."

They were standing in the large hall, and Judith instinctively took a step backward. Everything in her wanted to distance herself from that idea. Those lovely children, with their large, trusting eyes were the last thing she needed at this moment.

"Let Paula take care of her own children," she snapped. "She is not the only one who has had an emotional week."

"She is expecting another baby, Judith," he explained, struggling to be patient with her suddenly nasty tone.

This revelation hit Judith right between the eyes. Paula was expecting another baby. Again the rage welled in her. She had to avert her eyes to hide her anger from Harro, but he turned her face toward him.

"You're not jealous are you?" he asked, as though a light had just gone on. "Please be reasonable, Judith," he continued. "Rein and Paula have been married for years. We have only been married a few months. You must be patient. Our time will come."

Judith fought the tears.

"You're not jealous?" he had asked.

If she had sensed in those words something of the teasing tenderness with which he had encircled her from the very beginning, she would have perhaps laid her head on his shoulder and readily admitted, "Yes, Harro, I am jealous. I am so jealous that I am drowning in it, and with good reason."

But there was no tenderness in his voice, just veiled irritation.

She forgot her good intentions and processed the pain at that unexpected news about Paula through an inconsiderate, sarcastic comment. "Yes, why should we be worried? After all, Rein is making sure that the family does not die away."

Then Harro said something that he had never before said to her. "Shut up!" he said with disdain. Then he turned and left.

When he returned that night, Judith already lay in bed.

She pretended to be sleeping, but Harro was not deceived. He came and sat on the edge of the bed and laid his hand against her face. He felt that her pillow was wet. "You have been crying."

She opened her eyes and looked at the alarm clock next to her. "Why are you so late? I waited until midnight."

"I was at the Warbler clearing up a few matters with Father. And then Charlotte cornered me. She has her problems, too. She had another fight, this time with Erik." He made a gesture to express his distaste.

"Why do they all come to you with their problems?" she asked.

He bent over to undo his shoes. "Maybe they think I have none of my own," he said ironically.

Judith looked at him from the corner of her eye. She could see the tired lines in his thin face and realized once again how much she loved him.

She timidly laid her hand on his sleeve. "Why did you walk away this evening?" she asked softly.

"I have no talent for fighting," he said curtly.

"I do," she admitted with shame. "I am sorry I was so mean to you, Harro."

He stood up and took a bottle of aspirin from the medicine cabinet hanging in their room.

As he filled his glass from the sink, he asked, "Is that why you were crying?"

"Now that Mother is dead," she said, beginning to cry, "everything has become so awful. It began when Lucy reacted so meanly to Inge. And now Charlotte with Erik, and you and I. It is like a spell was broken when she died."

"Stop that superstitious nonsense," he cut her off. "Everyone is nervous and out of sorts now that a whole winter of stress is over. But there is nothing else wrong."

He took the aspirin and began to undress.

"There is with me," Judith said wearily. "There is something wrong with me. I wanted so badly to talk with you the last few days, Harro, but there was never a chance. Time and time again you were called upon."

"You have had months to talk to me," he said with a hardness that she had never seen in him before, "but you let each opportunity go by. You have kept me waiting to the point where I began to doubt myself. And now suddenly you complain that I am not at your beck and call. Do you think you have chosen a good moment to reform your attitude? I understand that we must talk. But now it will be when I am ready."

Although his authoritarian tone pricked her pride, she felt put upon. "When . . . ," she began softly.

"Not the night before my mother's funeral, in any case," he quickly interrupted.

The funeral went by like a strange dream. The memory would be somewhat unreal for all those involved.

Everyone had a private memory of Marion and of the final mute gesture with which she said good-bye: the small, inspired smile that laid a bridge between heaven and earth.

When her body was entrusted to the grave, they understood how paradoxical this all was. They were torn by grief while at the same time believing that Marion had preceded them to a land where no one would ever say, "I am sick."

The next morning, Charlotte returned to Rome and Erik to Rotterdam. Inge would depart for Suriname in a few days.

It was very quiet in the Warbler.

During one of their brief visits to the Warbler Judith on impulse asked Reinier and Lucy if they would like to come to the House of Herewaarden for dinner on Sunday. Harro gave her a look of indebtedness.

It was the first time that they had had contact after that strange night conversation.

When they returned home, Harro went to his desk; she, however, was driven outside by her unrest.

She wandered the castle gardens where the forsythia had begun to blossom, and a little further up, the rhododendrons in white, pink, dark red, and lavender. The hedges had in some places attained a height of several yards and formed a dark, mysterious forest.

Harro had told her that Rein and he used to play with their friends here. She could vividly envision how the dark pathways between the gnarled branches and trunks must have spoken to the imagination of the boys.

She plucked one of the dark red flowers and looked attentively at the stamens in the heart of the flower.

Her thoughts wandered.

As if in a mirror, she saw herself standing against the background of the winding hedges, healthy and in full flower, a ripe woman with shining hair and full red lips.

She plucked at the petals in her hand; the fiery petals floated aimlessly toward her feet.

Ornamental hedges, she thought, just like me. *They blossom but bear no fruit.*

She had not heard Harro approaching her. He had followed her after a few moments, but the thick grass carpet had cushioned his steps.

She jumped from fear when he, standing behind her, suddenly wrapped his arms around her.

"If you were ever in any doubt," she heard his voice, close to her ear, say, "I love you. Now tell me what it is that is bothering you so."

She lowered her head. "There is something wrong with me. I cannot have children," she confessed wearily.

"No!" he said, as though he were casting the very thought as far from himself as possible.

"I know it for certain," she held fast.

He gripped her wrists and turned her roughly around so he could look into her eyes.

"You went to a doctor without telling me?"

Judith blinked nervously. "It is worse than you think, Harro. I have known it for years. To be precise, five years and seven months."

She saw him thinking, putting things together, and understanding.

His face became taut, with the same inaccessibility that his father had shown during the last few days of grief and extreme control: a face of stone. His hard fingers continued to press her wrists.

"Come on," he said sternly.

❧ Chapter 21 ❧

They walked back to the house, and until they reached the confines of their own quarters, they spoke not a word.

"Sit down," he said, and she obeyed.

He went to a cabinet and poured them both a glass of sherry, purposely dragging out the silence in order to collect his thoughts. One by one, her formerly incomprehensible actions and words began to make sense for him. Her sudden departure from Constantine. Her declaration to Mrs. Von Braun: "I would stand in the way of his happiness, and I don't want that." Her sad confession in Nijmegen: "My dream is dead." The words she had wrestled out of herself on the viewing tower: "I must tell you something first, Harro." Her alarm when she met the man who once played the leading role in her life, in the company of a wife and two children. The bitter distaste in her expression when she heard about Rein and Paula's new baby.

As the pieces of the puzzle fell into place, he was left with but one question: Why had she circumvented the truth for so long?

He brought her her glass and said with a touch of irony, "Here, drink something. You will need it."

"What are you planning to do?" she asked, vainly attempting to answer his jest.

"I want an explanation from you," Harro said, suddenly harsh, "and I hope that just this once you will do no violence to the truth."

His words hit her hard.

She was prepared for his anger; she had intended to accept every reasonable accusation from him. But submission was one quality that was foreign to her nature, and now that it came down to it, she broke out against him in anger. "I did not lie to you!"

"Must I refresh your memory?" he asked with a quick, dangerous flicker of his piercing look.

She knew that he was thinking of their intimate conversations in which she had woven her dreams into his, even though she knew all too well that they contained not a speck of reality.

She understood how deceived and hurt he must feel.

"I did my utmost to spare you this, Harro," she defended herself passionately. "You know that as well as I do. But you just had to marry me. Before we were engaged I tried twice to tell you everything, but you made me stop, you wanted so badly to play Don Quixote!"

Again she saw the pain in his eyes and regretted the fact that she was not able to keep her sharp tongue under better control.

The accusation in his answer unleashed in her a bloodless laugh. "I had not considered such a possibility." He frowned. "And how could I? You consciously misled me into thinking that it was a man who ruined your life."

"If only I had misled you," she said bitterly. "I concede that it is more than enough for a girl of twenty-three to find out from a specialist that she is infertile. But what do you think of a man who makes his wedding dependent on the results of a medical test? The first two years he profits from the youth and adoration of his fiancée, only to push her aside without scruple because she cannot deliver an heir for the family firm that had become an idol for him. Isn't that enough to be destroyed by, Harro Van Herewaarden?"

Harro turned very pale. "What a rotten, cowardly thing to do!" he said, biting off his words. He wanted to walk to her, to take her in his arms, to comfort her, and to kiss away the tears welling up in her eyes. But the barricade that had risen between them obstructed him. He remained where he was, but the edge was no longer in his voice.

"Why didn't you trust me, Judith?" he asked with difficulty. "Why did you think that I would abandon you the same way? That was what you were afraid of, wasn't it?"

"At first I was," she began, faltering. "I was skeptical of all men, Harro. You must understand that. Why would you have accepted me if you had known everything?"

"For a very pertinent reason—for a Don Quixote," he added with irony. "For love. Did I not make it clear enough to you that I loved you for who you were? It seems to me that you should have taken the risk of laying your cards on the table."

"But I wanted to!" she cried. "When I was here in Borg for the first time, I was about to tell you everything, but you said to me, 'Do you think that I would love you less if I knew?' That is what you said, Harro, word for word, and I said no. I said no, because I trusted you, even then. And every day since then I have grown to love you more!"

Her hard-won self-control began to cave in. Her nostrils flared, and she swallowed with difficulty. Then she laid her head against the high back of the chair and broke down into sobs.

Harro stood looking at her, torn by inner conflict. His heart went out to her, but his injured pride stuck in his throat.

When he finally called her name, she stood up, blinded by her tears. Everything in her longed to bridge the gulf between them, but she took no more than one step, the reserve in Harro's voice holding her back.

"Sit down," he said, unrelenting. "We are not finished talking yet. So you have grown to love me more each day. But apparently that did not prevent you from pulling the wool over my eyes. You just had to have doll curtains in the children's room, huh? And I would be such an ideal father. May I please know why that whole charade was necessary?"

His scorn cut deep.

She was now so shattered that she gave up looking for explanations for her behavior that would be acceptable to him.

She only knew the simple truth, and this she gave to him, shaking and sobbing. "You were so happy, so carefree. I could not bear the thought of causing you grief, shattering your dreams. I wanted you to have your own family so desperately, little blond children who would look and laugh just like you.

"That was also the only reason I walked away from you in Constantine. But you were so persistent, Harro. The temptation was too great; I could not resist. When it became clear to me that you were not going to give up on me, it seemed to make little sense to tell you what was wrong with me. Even if I could not give you a child, at least I could let you have your illusion for a time."

He could not shake the feeling that he had been made a fool of, locked out of his own affairs, like an immature child.

With an irritated movement he removed his glasses and

began to polish them. All the while he weighed the word, *illusion* for its worth, and came to the conclusion that it was empty and bitter as gall.

"That all sounds very well and good," he said finally with a cold tone, "but that is the way you pacify a child, with bubbles and fairy tales. That is not the way you conduct a marriage, Judith."

He emptied his glass and walked away.

But before he could reach the door, she called him back. "Harro! Don't leave! I feel so miserable."

He turned around. "How do you think I feel? May I please be alone for a while to think things over?"

She bent her head.

When the door had closed behind him, she clung desperately to certain words of Inge: "He cannot become so angry that his love will not win in the end."

Harro stayed outside for a long time.

The twilight of the spring evening became ever darker, until it was completely dark.

Judith did not know what to do, except go to bed. Slowly, deep in thought, she undressed, recoiling from the moment when Harro would return and at the same time longing for it.

When she left the bathroom, pulling the door shut behind her, he suddenly returned, without her hearing him. He gripped her wrists with the same roughness of a few hours before and pulled her to himself. By the dim light of the reading lamp above the bed, her eyes found his—the eyes of an injured man.

She looked him directly in the eyes. "What are you going to do?"

"I'm going to teach you once and for all that I am no boy."

❧ Chapter 22 ❧

The next morning, as Judith made preparations for the meal, Inge suddenly appeared next to her in the kitchen.

She would be leaving for the airport that afternoon to begin her trip back to Suriname, but they had already said good-bye the evening before.

"I know we have already said farewell," Inge explained her unexpected entrance, "but I wanted to see the House of Herewaarden just one more time before I left. It will be a long time before I return—if ever."

Judith nodded. "I spoke with Harro last night," she said bluntly.

She continued with her work while Inge tried to measure her mood.

"How did he take it?" Inge probed with caution.

"Not well," said Judith concisely. "I have never seen him like that."

"Like what?"

Judith's hands ceased their busyness for a moment while she searched for the right words.

"So merciless," she replied.

"That doesn't sound like Harro," Inge said. "You should be able to expect at least a modicum of understanding from him."

Judith turned toward her with a quick movement. "I don't want you saying that! I have treated him shamefully, and I am not sure I could have respected him if he had just taken it all lying down. He had every right to be angry."

Inge bit back a smile creeping onto her lips at the fact that Judith was now defending her husband so intensely.

"You must have had a couple of awful days."

Judith nodded grimly. "If you knew how many quick prayers I have sent up since that conversation with you. I had come clean with God, and I was hoping that He would show me the right way and give me the right words. But I apparently have a great deal to learn about obedience and surrender. At crucial moments my temper got away from me and I became harsh and said the wrong things."

Inge jumped up from the table. Her time was limited.

"It will be all right," she said reassuringly. "To put it in medical jargon, this was a major operation that was necessary to remove a cancerous part of your relationship. Major operations usually leave painful wounds that do not heal immediately. You must give him some time, Judith."

Inge gave her a spontaneous kiss on the cheek. "I really must be going, but my thoughts will be with both of you. You must believe that."

Judith smiled in gratitude. "I am so happy we met, Inge," she said, deeply indebted. "Have a safe return and my best wishes, especially for little Marion." She accompanied Inge to the door.

"Where is Harro?" Inge asked.

"In the orchard next door. They are busy spraying for something or other."

Inge nodded. "I'll find him."

Judith watched her as she walked through the garden, consciously avoiding the paths. She wondered what she would say to Harro. She had not dared to ask.

Inge sniffed with delight the smell of the fresh, dew-covered grass into which her feet sank. She bent over and picked a buttercup.

How many times she had yearned for these things in the years gone by.

She thought somewhat philosophically that it appeared to be her lot in life to move from one homesickness to another. It was the price she paid for having the riches of homes in two worlds.

Harro saw her approaching. He met her at the boundary between the orchard and the gardens. "Is something the matter?" he asked, puzzled.

"I wanted to see the castle one more time before I left," she said truthfully. He made a royal gesture. "Go where you will. You know the way."

"I have been with Judith," she said.

His face grew tight. "Well, from the way in which you said that, I assume she has told you?"

"Last week," she admitted. "I can't tell you how bad I feel for you, Harro," she continued, "and I understand that you can't get over it just like that. But do me a favor and show a little compassion for Judith. What you say and do means so much to her."

Harro looked at her hostilely. "Are you trying to defend her?"

"Make no mistake, Harro. I have learned enough in my life to know that extraordinary circumstances require extraordinary solutions. I have raked her over the coals, but I have also encouraged her and prayed for her. Judith has many miserable, lonely years behind her," she concluded sincerely, "but now she is making her way with fits and starts back to God, and you must not stand in her way."

He made an impatient gesture. "You may be right, but I am afraid that I am in no position to evangelize right now."

Inge looked at his unhappy face and felt sorry for him. "Everyone has some cross to bear, Harro," she warned, "although I must admit that your baptism by fire has come at a very difficult moment, so soon after Mother's death."

She looked attentively at the flower in her hand, estimating how much he could bear. Then she lifted her face toward him and smiled into his stern eyes, a smile full of the ironic wisdom of life.

"You have always been an excellent mediator, Harro—for others. Try to see into yourself with as much insight and style, now that you are one of the feuding parties. If you happen to read your Bible soon, read First Corinthians thirteen. It is an educational chapter."

"You should have been a lawyer," Harro said.

She reached her hand to him with a disarming gesture.

"I am, in my spare time," she said.

Behind her jesting words he tested her urgent sincerity that was calling on the best in him. Inge and he had always had a soft spot for each other, and he saw little chance of closing himself completely to her open face.

"Your plea was not too bad, for an amateur," he said with a touch of humor, for the first time surrendering something of his reserve. "You will be hearing from us, Inge—one way or another."

She would have to make do with that.

That afternoon Reinier brought Inge to the airport. They took the same route as when he had picked her up, but now in the opposite direction.

They both had the feeling that not weeks, but months had passed since then. Without many words, they sat next to each other while the Chevrolet put the miles behind them.

Reinier was occupied with his memories, and Inge thought of Bram, who no doubt was looking forward to her return. Suddenly she longed so desperately to feel his arms around her once again and to press the warm bodies of her children against her. On impulse, she promised herself that she would never leave them for such a long time again.

She saw little Marion lying in her little bed so clearly that it seemed more real than imagination. The thin, pale mouth with the funny, sharp baby teeth, the always damp blond curls, the weak, thin little body that simply would not thrive. Inge had long ago lost count of the times that she had prayed heaven to preserve this child for them and give her fragile health a reprieve.

But now for the first time she realized with a jolt of consternation that her prayers made little sense as long as she continued to refuse to make use of the means that might lead to the recovery of the baby.

Bram had said that she should send little Marion to Holland, and Bram would not have said that if it were not urgently necessary.

She not only had complete trust in his diagnosis, she also knew he loved his children and was very attached to them. Bram would suffer just as much from a separation as she would—and yet he had spoken the harsh words, harsh words that she had for weeks now pushed to the back of her mind. It could be little Marion's salvation to grow up in Holland, far from the suffocating heat of the jungle that was undermining her tender life.

"Leave little Marion in the Netherlands?" she had shouted at the time. "I won't do it Bram. I will never do it! I can't be without her!"

"Maybe it simply has to be done precisely because we can't be without her," his answer had been.

He had not wanted to force her, and she remembered her relief when he had not pressed her.

But now, in this stunning moment of insight, she came to the razor-sharp realization that the risk she was taking was greater than she could justify. The life of a child was too precious to sacrifice for the instinctive urge of a mother to keep her chicks under her wings.

Bram had seen it before she had.

She thought how easy it was to moralize where others were concerned but how difficult it was to face one's own problems.

Why did it have to be on her trip home that she came to this realization?

Frantically she asked herself whether there was still something she could do to make up for her oversight.

Judith came to mind, and the words with which she said good-bye: "Best wishes, especially for little Marion."

Judith, with her empty hands that so desperately wanted to hold her own little Marion. The solution to both of their problems was so obvious that she did not understand why she had not seen it earlier.

Reinier had been observing his daughter. "This has been no vacation for you, has it?" He interrupted the long silence.

She gave him a sidelong glance, somewhat confused. "Why do you say that?"

"You look so worried. Can I do something to make you happier, my child?"

She looked at him with a peculiar expression.

"Maybe you can," she said with her deep, raspy voice, and she bravely swallowed the pain in her throat. What she was about to say would make everything so irrevocable, but it had to be done.

"Would you ask Harro and Judith if they would take in our little Marion, Father?"

He had to think through that request for a moment. "Because of her health?" he asked.

She nodded.

"If we keep her with us, sooner or later she will succumb to the climate," she said softly. Her lips trembled.

Reinier laid a warm, comforting hand on her hair. From the simple fact that she had waited until the last moment to bring up the subject, he understood how hard it was for her.

"I know from experience what it is like to be separated from your child, Inge," he said. "You don't have to be strong for me."

Two large tears welled in her eyes. "Bram wanted me to bring her along," she explained, "but I was not ready for that, Father. And now that I finally see he was right, I am on the way home."

She used her handkerchief before she went on. "If Judith and Harro will take her in, getting her to Borg is still a major problem. You can't just send a child of a year and a half through the mail." She smiled sadly.

"That is a practical difficulty, but it has nothing to do with the fact that you must send her so far away," Reinier offered.

Accustomed as he was to solving business problems in a quick and efficient way, he already had a proposal.

"One of us could fly to Paramaribo soon," he said, "and if you think it would be too difficult for the little lady to make the trip down the river, we could charter a helicopter for that leg of the journey."

Inge looked at him, tenderly laughing to herself. "Do you know what that would cost?" she asked soberly.

"No," he said stubbornly, "but it doesn't matter."

"You are the nicest old fool I know," Inge said affectionately, and he grinned with satisfaction.

Since her arrival in Holland, Inge had not seen him so contented. They talked over a few practical matters, and then they arrived at the airport.

"What will Bram say about all this?" Reinier wondered. "We have really improvised, haven't we?"

No matter how he looked at it, it was not his place to arrange these things without his son-in-law, even though he realized that communication with the remote mission post was difficult, unless they were willing to waste precious time.

"Our lives there depend on improvisation," Inge said, "but in this case it is different. The decision to board little Marion was first made in principle by Bram, months ago. What you and I have done is to give practical form to that decision. I give you *carte blanche,* Father, and you don't have to worry about Bram. He knows better than anyone how necessary it is to send little Marion out of there."

She bit her lip. Now and again it was too much for her, and yet she was relieved to have cut through the knot once and for all, denying herself the chance to crawl back.

Oddly enough, she felt no doubts about how Harro and Judith would view these matters.

When the formalities were behind them and they had only to wait for the plane, Reinier said, in a thoughtful moment, "Harro and Judith. Was there any particular reason you chose them?"

She nodded, knowing she was in an awkward position. Would she be breaking confidence if she were to share Judith's sorrow with her father?

Reinier saw her hesitate. He remembered the silent concern that Marion had harbored for these two until the day she had died.

"Should I go this evening?" he probed. "Or are things still pretty rough?"

Inge nodded again. "Maybe it would be better if you waited a few days," she decided.

"You are speaking in riddles, but I will control my curiosity."

"They will tell you themselves," she said.

She thought of the crisis in that young marriage, of her own wrestling of the last hours, of her father's glaring loss.

She laid her cheek against his furrowed face, not caring who saw her. "Father," she said, seeking his help as though she were still that young girl of thirteen years ago, "life is sometimes hard, isn't it?"

"Hard, Inge?" he replied. "Yes, it is. But it is well worth it."

❦ Chapter 23 ❧

Harro and Judith had coexisted in silence practically the entire day, consciously avoiding eye contact.

Judith felt they were simply postponing hostilities, and she was deeply unhappy.

That evening, Lucy came by.

She had returned to school for the first time and had a few problems with her homework. Harro helped her with them, patiently repeating the same thing three and four times whenever her disinterested mind could not concentrate on the material at hand.

Judith sat with a book she was not reading. She was envious of the attention her husband was devoting to his sister.

At ten o'clock, Harro took Lucy back home. He asked Judith not to come along to the Warbler, and she was too proud to beg. She had nothing else to do, but her memory of the previous evening prevented her from going to bed.

She decided to visit Diederick and Juliette.

The western wing, however, appeared to be dark already. Slowly and circuitously, she wound her way back through the gardens, discontented and aggrieved.

At the landing of the main entrance to the castle, she slowed her pace. She laid her hand on the head of one of the kindly looking lions positioned at the sides of the steps and asked herself how old these carvings could be. Harro would no doubt be able to tell her, but it really didn't matter.

She sat on the landing, her arm draped around the cold lion's head. *Harro's proper grandmother would have a fit of indignation if she saw me sitting here,* she thought with a touch of irony.

It was a beautiful mild evening. The moon shone on the lawns and on the paths lined with white gravel, leaving the shadows beyond just that much darker.

It made her think of something Inge had said: "Go out into the darkness and put your hand in the hand of God."

Judith's thoughts began to roam.

After a while, she saw Harro coming up the approach road. She recognized him from the way he carried himself long before she could hear the white stones grinding under the soles of his shoes.

As he approached, he noticed her, but rather than making some surprised or irritated comment about the strange place she had chosen to sit, he sat down next to her.

The fact that he did that—even in the absence of their old intimacy—lent her a certain comfort in her loneliness.

She listened to the distant mournful cries of a farm dog and the screech of a night owl, sensing that she ought not break this loaded silence with triviality.

Finally it was Harro who spoke. "Inge has been an outstanding lawyer for the defense," he said.

She turned to see his face. "I did not ask her to plead my case," she answered with dignity. "I want you to realize that."

He was irritated by her unflinching tone, forgetting that it was precisely her spirit that had from the very beginning most attracted him to her.

"You could use a good lawyer," he reacted sharply.

Judith pushed her nails into her palms in order to avoid blurting out a hostile response.

She stood up and said with the same quiet confidence of a moment before, "You have it wrong, Harro. No one has to bother to argue my case because I declared myself guilty a long time ago. The next step is yours."

He, too, stood up, with the feeling that all his weapons had been taken from him. She had confessed her guilt and delivered herself to him for better or worse. He had only two possibilities open to him: continue to punish her by giving in to his cold, injured pride or forgive all her pretenses and lack of trust with the greatest gesture required of him by the measure of his love. And if he seriously considered himself a Christian, there was not even a choice.

He simply had to put a period behind everything that had happened and take up together with her the cross that had been laid on them.

All these things ran through him in the twinkling of an eye.

Judith stood on the first level of the landing, he on the ground.

Their eyes were level with each other during these seconds, which were filled to overflowing with inner doubt and prayer.

Judith plumbed his dark expression.

The smoldering rage that had so frightened her the previous evening had left him. She dared to timidly lay her hand on his arm.

It seemed to Harro that their roles had been reversed.

From the injured party, it suddenly now appeared that he had become the offender.

He pursed his lips as though in pain.

"I am not ready for that yet," he said with difficulty. "I'm sorry."

She withdrew her hand. Oddly enough, she no longer felt sad and defeated.

"You must give him some time," Inge had said.

"Maybe it is my turn to patient," she simply stated.

It was, nevertheless, not easy to live with Harro in this situation. Although he was obliging and polite, although he no longer accused her, he was so quiet—so disturbingly quiet.

During the night on Saturday she had a nightmare in which she wandered alone, seeking someone like herself, a companion—a voice that spoke, a hand that supported, a heart, an open ear. It was an old, vexing dream from which she awoke with a cry.

Harro was very sweet to her; he brought her something to drink and held her for a long time silently against himself, until her frightened shudders ceased.

"Have you had this dream before?" he wanted to know.

"At first a lot," she said softly. "Also when I was in Pakistan. But not after that. I got used to it."

"To what?"

"To the feeling of abandonment." She shivered.

He took it personally that this frightening dream had returned just now. "You do not have to feel abandoned," he said curtly.

"Are you sure?" she asked defenselessly.

The words cut through him. "It is one of the few things of which I am absolutely certain," he affirmed. He tucked her in like a small child. "Go back to sleep. I'll leave the light on. You never have to be afraid."

The next morning he let her sleep in and went to church alone.

When he returned, his father was with him, and Lucy.

Judith poured coffee and made herself busy with the meal,

but her mind was still occupied with the events of the previous night.

When she was able to get Harro alone for a moment, she
said with shame, "I believe that I behaved rather ridiculously
last night."

"There was nothing to laugh about," he said generously.
"On the contrary."

Their guests stayed the entire day. Reinier and Lucy stayed
to eat and did not have the slightest desire to return to the
deadness of the Warbler.

In the afternoon, Erik arrived unexpectedly from Rotterdam. When he found no one at the Warbler, he called Harro.
"Do you know where Father is?"

"With us on the patio," Harro said laconically, "behind a
cold glass of lemonade. If you come over, you can get one,
too."

Erik was there within five minutes, and Diederick and Juliette arrived at the same time. They sat in the sun and comforted one another with their company in order to numb the
pain of the void left by Marion's departure.

Reinier looked around the circle surreptitiously.

"You can bet that things will stay like this," he said confi-
dentially to Judith, who sat next to him. "Now that the Warbler has fallen silent, your home will become more and more
a central point and magnet. I know myself and my children
and brother; people like us are irresistibly attracted to happiness and companionship, and a house without a wife is a
house without a soul."

Judith's eyes brimmed with confusion. "How could I ever
take Mother's place?" she asked doubtfully.

He shrugged his shoulders. "Time will prove me right," he
stubbornly maintained.

"I hope so," she said softly.

The following evening Reinier returned by himself; this

time to talk about his granddaughter. He had stuck closely to Inge's instructions and waited a few days, but now there were bridges to build.

"I have a message for you two from Inge," he said as he entered. "She asked whether you two would be willing to take on her little Marion."

Harro threw a quick glance at his wife and wondered how she would handle this. He remembered the contrived manner in which she always kept the children of Rein and Paula at a distance, in spite of their loving affection—or perhaps because of it.

A nervous pull fell over Judith's face. "For good?" she asked breathlessly.

"That is what it amounts to," her father-in-law affirmed. "The constitution of the child is not up to life in the jungle. It cost Inge a great struggle to acknowledge that, but she finally managed to muster the courage. I am very proud of her, you should know. It is quite something to willingly give up a child."

While he was still speaking, Judith stood up and walked quickly out of the room.

Reinier looked quizzically at his son. "Did I say something wrong?"

Harro shook his head. "Leave her for a moment. She has been out of sorts of late."

He looked the other full in the face. "We will never have our own children, Father," he declared.

Instantly everything became very clear to Reinier. "And Inge knew it," he concluded.

He realized as he had never before the wealth he possessed in his six children. He looked at the pinched face of his son and tried in vain to put himself in his place.

Harro confirmed his conclusion. "Yes, Inge knew." A disturbing thought suddenly occurred to him. "She isn't doing this just for us, is she?"

"Not in the least," his father assured him. "Before Inge left for the Netherlands, Bram urged her to bring the baby along, but she couldn't let her go. During her stay with us, she pushed the thought of the separation out of her mind until the very last minute. But I assume that her familiarity with your grief did indeed influence her decision. What is your inclination in this matter, Son?"

"Positive," Harro said immediately. "You know how much I care about Inge," he continued. "Her children will always be welcome in the House of Herewaarden. That goes without saying, but especially in this case. Caring for a weak and helpless little doll like Marion Dubois could be the best medicine in the world for Judith, and Inge apparently saw that, too."

He stood up. "You won't mind if I go to her now?"

He found Judith in the kitchen, where she stood in front of the window, staring at nothing in particular.

He laid his hand on her shoulder.

"We have certainly received more than we even asked for, haven't we?" he said, with a subtle irony that was unique to him, but her keen ears detected the emotion in his voice.

"Can we accept this, Harro, things being what they are between us at the moment?"

It touched and shamed him that she had been so sensitive to this and had brought it up as a point for consideration.

"Inge knew what she was doing," he proposed.

"I don't get it," she said hurt. "Would you be willing to hand your child over to a couple that you left behind in such absolute discord—to avoid simply calling it a fight?"

"Probably not," he honestly confessed, "unless I was deeply convinced that they loved each other enough."

"What is enough?" she asked doubtfully.

Harro pursed his lips. He thought of the Bible passage to which Inge had called his attention during their conversation in the orchard. The content of the passage he remembered fairly clearly: Love is patient, love is kind, it is not rude, it is not self-seeking, it is not easily angered, it keeps no record of wrongs, it always protects, always hopes, always perseveres.

He remembered down to the very details what had taken place between them over the last few days. He did not see much of himself when he used this perfect mirror.

Absolutely, Judith, he thought. *What is enough? We have only made a small beginning in true love. And yet God gives us this new chance.*

Overcoming himself, he threw his arms around her and buried his face in her neck. "Judith," he said, subdued, "Judith, darling, let's try it together. This must have been arranged for us from above."

❧ Chapter 24 ❧

When they finally entered the sitting room again, Reinier noticed at a glance that everything was all right between them.

"While you two had your tête-à-tête and lost track of time, I took the liberty of helping myself to a cigar," he said to his son, ignoring Judith's red eyes.

"Some people really push their rudeness to extremes," Harro replied, with the same reckless tone of voice.

Judith was happy to hear them playing with each other, but she knew them well enough to recognize that this time they were not paying much attention.

She went and sat by the low table and made an impatient gesture that wiped all other words from the slate.

"Let Father tell us about it now," she said. "How are we going to be able to bring little Marion here?"

"I may assume, then, that you are prepared to take responsibility for her?" Reinier said.

"Yes," Harro answered for both of them, "we are."

"I would have gladly taken her myself," Reinier confessed. "I would have been proud to have a Marion under the roof of the Warbler again. But I am too old, and Lucy is too young to raise a child. It is good that Inge set her sights on you." He paused for a moment and puffed his cigar.

"And now about your question," he said to Judith. "One of us three should go to Suriname to pick up the little one. There is no other solution. I will, of course, pay the costs."

"How much time would it take?"

"A few weeks, at least, maybe longer. Inge left me the addresses of a couple of contacts in Paramaribo, friends of Bram who would be happy to assist us. Harro knows from experience how much preparation is required for such a trip to the mission post. It is not even possible to buy a return ticket."

The young couple looked at each other rather indecisively, wondering whether Reinier himself might want to make the trip. If someone had to go, he, of course, had the first right to go.

Harro cut through the knot and asked Reinier directly.

"Of course I would like to get acquainted with my grandchildren there," Reinier said, "with Jaques and Marie-Louise, and Reina, and the bush people whom I know only from letters and the stories of Inge. If there was no other solution, I would not hesitate to go there. But as things stand now, I think it would be best if I were to care first for my own single children, who will certainly miss their mother a lot in the endless summer break that is almost here. If it is all the same to you, I would rather not close the Warbler this summer."

They understood. Their father still had a responsibility, and they respected him for not closing himself off to the others in his grief.

"If anyone comes to mind to pick her up, it would be Judith," Harro gave his opinion, "not least because she can most easily break away from here, and it seems to me a kind gesture to give little Marion the chance to get acquainted a little with her adoptive mother in her own familiar environment.

"The transition will be shocking enough for her. And don't we owe it to Bram, too? The least he could wish is to meet the person to whom he is entrusting his child."

"There is no flaw in that argument," Reinier admitted. "What do you think, Judith?"

"I would like to," she said simply.

"Wouldn't you rather have Harro go along?"

"Of course, but he is up to his ears in work."

No one could deny it, but Reinier was not satisfied with that. "Can you handle it?" he continued to press. "It is definitely not a comfortable journey through the interior. You will have to take on responsibilities and make decisions without having a second opinion to fall back on."

Judith turned bright red. "In some ways I am a potential coward," she said honestly, "but I think I will be able to muster the necessary courage."

"She has tamed snakes in Pakistan and polar bears in Alaska," Harro said. "You must not think that I have married an inexperienced woman, Father."

For the first time there was something of the old, teasing twinkle in his eye, which Judith secretly noted with a shiver of happiness.

The time went by unnoticed, with all there was to discuss.

When Reinier finally left and the door fell closed behind him, Judith and Harro stood across from each other in the room, not sure what to do with their sudden intimacy. An unmistakable shyness hovered between them that appeared difficult to overcome.

This evening had undeniably brought them closer to-gether, but they both intuitively felt the impossibility of sim-ply falling back into their old pattern as though nothing had happened.

The memory of the power struggle of that night on which he indeed appeared to come out as a winner, but lost some-thing essential of himself by acting as a brute, was still too painful for Harro.

And the awareness that for the four endless days and nights since that evening Harro had left her out in the cold, con-sciously avoiding her desire for contact—with the sole excep-tion of those few unreal moments after she had awakened from her nightmare—was still too fresh in Judith's mind.

But this evening he had thrown his arms around her in a moment of great sincerity, and later he had teased her, some-thing of his trusted, painfully absent smile apparent deep in his eyes.

She clung to these things when the silence got too much for her. In order to give herself something to do, she began to collect dirty coffee cups, but Harro decreed, "Do that tomor-row. The meeting is adjourned."

After his comment, however, he fell back into the silence to which he had grown accustomed over the past few days.

Somewhat later, as Judith brushed out her hair, as was her custom, she broke the silence between them with a question.

"Does your father know?"

He did not need to ask what she meant. "Yes, he knows."

"From Inge?"

"No, I told him myself."

"Did you have to?"

Their eyes met in the mirror. Then he said decidedly, "Let's make one thing perfectly clear, Judith, before you be-gin playing hide and seek with others: There is no reason for you to be ashamed that you cannot have children, and there is no reason to try to hide it. After all, you did not make yourself this way."

There was again a trace of irritation in his voice that left her feeling despondent. *If only he understood,* she thought, exasperated.

She continued brushing her hair with slow, methodical strokes; sparks crackled as she brushed.

"I know," she answered him softly. "With my mind I know you are right. But it is more than just my mind that speaks, Harro. There is something in me that simply does not accept that reasoning. It is stubborn, too— the feeling of always being inadequate; for you, for your family, for the blossoming world outside, that ever and again produces its fruit."

She made a helpless gesture.

In one way or another, it was very important that he understand what she meant.

"I don't know how I can explain it to you," she resumed. "Maybe you would only understand if the roles were reversed and the fact that we could have no children fell to your account. That does sometimes happen you know, Harro."

He had never looked at it in that way.

She is right, he knew, flabbergasted. *I would not be able to bear the thought. I would probably be just as oversensitive and vulnerable as she is.*

He underwent a moment of repentance and understood, in an extremely painful confrontation with himself, that he was at this moment even more unbearable for her than he had been during his rage of the previous week.

Never before had he considered himself so mercilessly: The victim who was graciously prepared to assume a generous disposition. He had no right to prescribe for her a mode of conduct for which she was not yet ready. He would have to climb down from his pedestal and participate in her need.

Finally he came to the same conclusion as he had before, on

the landing. Together, falling down and getting up again, they would have to find a way that would lead to the acceptance of this common grief. He knew it back then, but he was not ready to give in.

Again they found each other's eyes in the mirror.

"Judith, darling," he began, humbly.

She immediately sensed the change in his voice and turned to him in a sudden, spontaneous movement. The brush fell from her hand, and Harro spanned the short distance that separated them with two strides.

"Judith, sweetheart," he began again.

It was the first time since she had known her husband that Judith had seen him at a loss for words.

He stood in front of her but did not touch her.

"I have been a perfect fool," he said gruffly. "I am sorry. If you do not want anything more to do with me, just say so. I would not blame you."

The corners of Judith's mouth curled up. "You're worse than a fool if you say such things. Give me a kiss, please. I am famished."

He pulled her to himself with a powerful sweep of the arm. Through her thin negligee he felt the willing warmth of her body and the beating of her heart.

Never had he been so aware of how much this woman meant to him, including her weakness and faults.

"You and I," he said fiercely. "You and I—and nothing in the world can change that!"

It sounded almost triumphant.

Deep in her eyes a light began to shine. She pulled his head down, and their lips found each other.

There were many things he wanted to say to her, but it did not matter anymore. Words could wait.

❦ Chapter 25 ❧

Marion's grave, in the old, rustic cemetery in Borg, had become a place of pilgrimage for all those who loved her.

Reinier and Lucy often walked there on the long, empty summer days when it could get so quiet at home.

The text on the large white marble tombstone was extremely sober. Her name, accompanied by the title she never used: MARION ELISABETH, BARONESS OF HEREWAARDEN; two dates—her birth and death—and under that a quote from a famous poem:

> Graves like empty nests
> From which a bird has flown heavenward.

Marion had spent her whole life amidst books and poems. Reinier had found in her dresser folders full of clippings and quotes, parts of novels that had for some reason or another struck her in a special way, and copied fragments of poetry.

He had divided them between Lucy and Harro, the only two in his family who had inherited their mother's passion for the written word.

Lucy had in the meantime passed her finals by the skin of her teeth. Although she brought a card of meager Cs home, she had managed to pass and finished high school.

Her father in one sense was concerned, yet was secretly very happy that she had decided to stay home for a few years to take on her mother's duties as much as possible.

Under the careful supervision of Toos, the housekeeping in the Warbler marched on without a hitch. But the things that make a house a home are intangible, and therefore could not be expected from Toos.

When Reinier imagined that Lucy would continue her studies as Inge and Charlotte had after they graduated, he shied away from the thought of the loneliness to which he would come home every night. It was his destiny—he knew it all too well—but he was thankful for the respite that had been granted him by the sweet affection of his youngest child.

It was early June when Judith left for Suriname to bring little Marion back to the Netherlands.

In the two weeks preceding her departure there were many preparations to be made. It was a wonderful sensation, after all that had happened and all the bitter words, still to be able to decorate a child's room on the sunny side of the castle.

When Judith was busy with the various tasks connected with the arrival of their niece, Harro would sometimes look up from what he was doing and observe her skillful hands.

When their eyes met, there was often a hint of shame in them, but now it was muted by the prelude to a new happiness.

Much was discussed between them in these weeks, and they gained from these conversations the knowledge that because of their limited possibilities, they, more than others, would have to find their happiness in each other.

One evening when Harro was busy sorting the papers left him by his mother, he found a short, unrhymed poem that he read and reread, only to tuck it in his wallet in the end.

Judith looked up from her sewing. "What was that?"

He smiled into her curious face. "That is a message that you will receive from me when you leave for Suriname."

"Why?"

"To help you hold on if you get another one of your scary dreams."

She had related to him the content of the nightmare that had pursued her for several months after Jan Willem Scheppers had betrayed her: a frightening image of extreme abandonment.

In the mental strain of the last few weeks the dream had returned, not just once, but several times.

Although their relationship was better than it had ever been, and Judith more and more felt that she had regained her balance, the enduring anxieties and fears apparently were still having their effect on her subconscious.

Harro sometimes teased her during the day about her "tricks," but when it came right down to it, he had an inimitable way of comforting her, and she knew him well enough to comprehend how deeply he felt about the fact that she was still so torn up inside by a conflict that had already been resolved.

His hint had raised her curiosity. She reached out her hand, "Let me see."

"Not a chance," he replied. "I am still available in the flesh if you need to hold on to something."

Judith could not help but think of this little incident as she stood at the point of saying farewell.

Harro had brought her to the airport and arranged everything.

She was rather nervous. Not because of the trip, she had flown many times before and liked it just fine. But the thought of being separated from Harro for such a long period of time did not excite her much, now that she was looking it in the face. They had agreed that she would spend at least three or four weeks at the mission post to ease the transition for little Marion, but that meant they would be apart a good share of the summer.

Harro held her hand tightly. "I want something from you," she said suddenly.

He kissed her. "Was that what you meant?"

"Definitely not. It is what you have in your wallet."

He laughed. "You are right. A promise is a promise." He pushed the little piece of paper into her purse. It was a clipping from a magazine, easily held in one hand.

Before they were over the North Sea, Judith knew it by heart:

When you lie alone at night
next to an awakened fear
of the immediate moment
in which no life is possible
but life without resonance,
of hollow where's and why's:

Write a check on skin and hair,
write a check on flesh and blood,
on breath and thought,
all will be redeemed
with the clinking coins of love.

For though we travel different horizons
we are but a breath away.

She had never had much interest in poetry, except perhaps when she was sixteen or so, but these lines put her at ease like a shot in the arm all the weeks that she was abroad. Harro knew exactly what she needed.

Six weeks later she returned to the Netherlands.

During her absence, Harro had moved into the Warbler, and it was there that he received the telegram from Paramaribo announcing her time of arrival.

His impatience drove him much too early to the airport.

An hour and a half before the plane arrived, he was there to pick her up. He drank too much coffee while he waited. He laughed at himself and wondered how his family could have labeled him the portrait of patience.

Finally the moment arrived.

The day was warm and almost without wind; Judith descended the stairs from the airplane in a light summer dress, little Marion on her arm.

Next to Judith's healthy, brown tint, the rather yellow skin of the thin, blond girl was immediately noticeable.

It was not difficult for Judith to spot Harro among those waiting. Because of his height, he stood out above the others.

Their eyes made but brief contact, and then it was not long before he had thrown his long arms around them both.

He took his time thoroughly greeting Judith, but before he was through, little Marion had managed to remove his glasses.

They laughed heartily, and it broke the ice.

Judith set the little girl on her feeble legs and the two of them squatted on both sides of her.

"This is now our little Marion," she said, and added to the child, "give Uncle Harro a kiss, sweetheart."

He carefully placed his large hands around her frail body.

She looked at him for a moment, then laid her face against his cheek in a touching gesture.

"Hawwo," she imitated.

"She is not scared of me at all," he said with surprise.

"What do you know!" Judith said. "The child has intuition!" On the way home, little Marion fell asleep in Judith's lap.

Over her head the two of them carried on in subdued voices a long and nearly constant conversation.

There was so much to tell of the long weeks that had passed between departure and return that they were in Borg before they knew it.

Paula and Lucy had arranged a welcome home party at the House of Herewaarden. A real Brabant buffet had been set up, and there were flowers everywhere one turned.

A brand-new high chair had been bought for little Marion. Judith blinked back her tears at all the affection. "How kind of you," she said, touched.

Lucy had taken over the baby and did not hear a word, but Paula giggled and threw her short, girlish hair back. "Harro said we could all come, on the condition that we let him go to the airport alone. You can understand why we could not refuse such an invitation. We are just happy that you are back safe and sound. Rein will be here soon, and Uncle Diederick and Aunt Juliette."

"Where did you leave the children?" Judith wanted to know.

"With a friend. It is busy enough as it is. I'll come with them again after little Marion has had a chance to adjust. She looks bewildered, doesn't she, the little dear?"

"And where is Father?" Judith inquired further.

"He went to pick up your mother from the train station," Paula announced.

"My mother? Did you ask her to come?"

Harro responded to her cry. "Blabbermouth!" he scolded Paula. "Can't you ever keep a secret?"

Judith silently compared this homecoming with that of a year ago, when she had felt like a stranger in her own land.

It felt wonderful.

And then Reinier entered with Mrs. Van Alkemade. First there was the business and the back and forth of the greetings, then he said with barely suppressed impatience to Judith, "And where is that little bundle that I had you make the trip for?"

Harro put a firm hand on his shoulder and directed him into a chair while Judith lifted the little girl from the floor and placed her on his knee.

He held her as though she were made of porcelain. "Marion," he said rather hoarsely.

It had become noticeably quiet in the room. The child looked at him with the alert dark eyes of her mother, then her mouth opened in surprised recognition. "Papa!" she said clearly.

The bystanders looked at one another with tender smiles.

"I feel overlooked," Harro said, breaking the heaviness.

Reinier looked around the circle. "What am I supposed to think of that?" he asked with amusement.

"You have, with all due respect, the same gray, weathered face and hair as her father," Judith solved the riddle. They all laughed.

"That is no compliment for Bram," Reinier conceded thoughtfully. "After all, we are seventeen years apart."

"If it is true that a tropical year counts for two, then he has almost caught up with you," Lucy quickly calculated, and they left it at that.

When everyone was finally present and they sat down at the table, another comic situation arose when little Marion refused to trade her grandpa's knee for the shiny new high chair.

"Now you must show her your authority," Judith teased her husband.

"But sweetheart, it was love at first sight between those two," he answered. "You don't think I am going to meddle in that, do you?"

"Is his position pedagogically proper? What do you think?" Judith asked Reinier. "You must know."

"A certain degree of tolerance in raising a child is permitted," he gave his concessive opinion.

Reinier grinned like a co-conspirator at his granddaughter. "I will buy you a rocking horse," he promised on impulse.

She tangled both hands in her hair and thought everything was good.

But Harro warned, "No extra presents, Grandpa. There is a limit to my tolerance."

With a lot of jesting and teasing, they took their places around the table.

Later, Judith passed around the pictures she had taken at the mission post and quickly had developed during her brief layover in Paramaribo.

Everyone had questions about her stay with Inge and Bram. After an hour, Harro noted that she had not yet had a bite to eat.

"And now eat!" he commanded, "or I will feed you."

When little Marion began to rub her eyes, the party broke up. No matter how celebrative this get-together might be, the child had to go to bed, and nothing could stand in the way of that.

It had been a long time since one of their family gatherings had been so saturated with such simple joy.

But all this was so much in the spirit of Marion that no one had the feeling that their cheerfulness—so few months after her death—was in any way out of place.

Before Reinier left for home, he took Judith to one side. A part of his heart was in Suriname, with his oldest daughter.

"I haven't heard you say anything about your departure from the mission post," he said. "Did Inge take the departure of little Marion pretty hard?"

Judith nodded seriously. "We'll talk another time privately about it, Father. I have not told nearly everything that there is to tell. You can understand why I did not want to put a damper on the festive mood. You don't know how wonderful it is to be received in such a spontaneous manner, especially when you have been on your own for so long, and have had so little to expect from the future. It was an unforgettable homecoming."

He nodded his understanding.

The confidence between them had now grown so much that he was able to express a thought that had been on his mind for several hours. "Do you know who would have enjoyed this party more than anyone?"

"Yes," said Judith, "I know."

Tears welled up in her eyes at the expression on his face. They did not have to name their grief to understand each other. She put her arms around him and hugged him. "Come more often," she said.

❧ Chapter 26 ❧

Mrs. Van Alkemade stayed the night at the House of Herewaarden.

When tranquility returned after everyone had gone his or her separate way, she said to her daughter and son-in-law, "It has been such a wonderful evening. If you two want to take a walk, I will take care of the baby."

"It sounds so unreal," Judith said.

"It is real," Harro corrected her. "From now on, we will need a baby-sitter if we want to go somewhere."

They gladly made use of the offer.

Mrs. Van Alkemade watched them as they entered the castle gardens in the falling darkness.

She was glad that she had accepted the invitation from the Van Herewaarden family to come from Wassenaar for this occasion. It had given her a deep sense of satisfaction to witness her daughter as the beaming center of attention.

For many years she had had her silent worries about this

child who had too quickly gone abroad and deprived herself of a mother's love at the very moment she most needed it.

She had read and reread the brief letters, which said little. She had sensed in them the unbroken disappointment and the growing cynicism, without knowing what to do.

And later, when Judith neglected to inform her fiancé about her inability to have children, her concern deepened.

She was painfully aware of the fact that she had little influence over the self-conscious young woman who was her daughter, and for months she had felt guilty toward Harro—made an accomplice against her will.

Before she left for Suriname, Judith had written her a long, openhearted letter that put an end to all her concerns.

Harro and Judith had in the meantime arrived at the woods, passing through the orchard.

It was very dark, but he knew the way blindfolded.

"Did you miss me?" Judith asked as he pulled her tenderly to himself.

He pinched her arm and she warned, "That will turn black and blue, I guarantee you."

"I don't care," he said heartlessly. "Confess. What were you and Father talking about alone?"

"About Inge. His heart goes out to her so, Harro. Everyone was happy today for our sake, but your father was aware of the other side of the coin. You have to be cut from hard wood to live the kind of life Inge and Bram have chosen," she went on.

"Or maybe I should say for which they have been chosen.

"Now that they have let go of little Marion, they have for the first time fully come to the realization that within ten years they will have to let go of their other children, as well.

"Jaques is nearly twelve; he will soon be going for at least five years to Paramaribo for junior high. He can still go home for a few months during the vacations, but when he is eighteen, he will have to come to the Netherlands to continue his studies. And in the meantime, the two girls will have grown up, and they would not want to deprive them of the possibilities for further developing themselves, either.

"But I imagine that it is very difficult for Inge to see that cloud looming on the horizon."

"So in a couple of years Jaques will also be coming here," said Harro pensively. "I remember him as a tough, lean little kid with an intractable will."

"He is a little Tarzan," Judith bettered, "but you should have seen how that tough little fellow got along with his little sister. He was more devastated by her departure than Marie-Louise and Reina. You know what he wanted me to ask you?"

"What?"

"Whether he can come live with us in the House of Herewaarden when he has to come to the Netherlands."

"He certainly is reserving a spot early enough," Harro said dryly. "What did you say?"

"That he was welcome, of course."

"You are sweet. First a baby, and now an up-and-coming student. Your life will be a little less peaceful than you once imagined."

"A peaceful life is the last thing I wanted for myself," Judith said. "I would rather become like your mother."

"Just be yourself," he advised. "That's better."

Her hand crept into his. "There is one more thing I have to tell you, Harro."

"What is it?"

"I spoke to Bram about the medical aspect of our problem."

Harro stood abruptly still. "Why?"

"Because I have seldom met such a well-rounded doctor who engenders in me the same confidence he does."

"I can understand that, but what did you expect to hear from him?"

"I wanted to know if it made any sense to submit to an operation."

She could feel the resistance in his disposition.

"I don't want you to undergo a lot of pain for a negligible chance of success," he said rather aggressively.

"Bram thought the chances were good," she came back.

"Did he examine you?" he asked.

"Yes."

"And did you tell him the conclusion of the gynecologist in Leiden?"

"Of course. And Bram fully agreed with his conclusion, but he spoke not of a one-in-a-thousand chance but of a one-in-ten chance. And that makes all the difference, Harro. He recommended that I consult a very qualified specialist in Brussels whose name he knows from medical journals. What do you think?"

Harro shrugged his shoulders. "I am not sure. You will never be able to avoid harboring hope, even though the chance of fulfilling that hope—even when viewed in this new light—remains extremely limited. I would rather spare you a second bitter disappointment, sweetheart.

"You, of course, will have to make your own decision, but you don't have to take the risk for me. I want you to know that."

Judith felt a deep sense of relief to hear him put it that way.

"We must take our time and think it over carefully," she said, and she surprised herself that she seemed to be ready to postpone these matters until a later date.

"We will certainly think it over," Harro agreed. "But you ought to know this much: Whether you do it or not, whether it helps or not, it will not change my feelings for you in the least. I love you, and all those other things, no matter how important, are secondary."

Only then did they continue on their way.

Their path led almost automatically to the viewing tower that had been the destination of countless other walks.

True to tradition, they climbed to the top.

It was not nearly as dark at the top as it was under the trees.

In the distance they could see lighted windows. They were the lights of the old house from which they had just come, the house that had seen more than twenty generations of Van Herewaardens grow up within its walls and now, after many years, again contained young life. On the other side was the Warbler, which also emitted its light. They could see the dark silhouette of the villa against the somewhat lighter background, and in the rear a warm, clear square of light.

They leaned over the railing, and Judith wondered out loud where the house had derived its name.

"Now that the Warbler has fallen silent . . . ," her father-in-law had said shortly after the death of his wife. She had never been able to completely forget those words.

Was the name a symbol? Had the little songbird once been a personification of happiness for him?

While they stood there and made their guesses, looking at that brightly lighted window, Reinier sat behind his desk and wrote a letter to Suriname.

As his fountain pen glided over the paper, relating to Bram and Inge the arrival of their daughter and how her grandfather had immediately been granted a place in her life, his heart lay continually with his own Marion, who had been taken from him and yet was with him still.

He felt bound not only to her, but also to the men and women they had left behind, with their children and grandchildren who each in turn would carry on the torch of their lives.

In an almost prophetic vision, he saw the centuries open before him. Man would go his own way. Progress would march on, further, always further, toward greater perfection, toward deeper knowledge and science, toward a spiral of war and violence, and toward more tears.

But faith and love would preserve their power.

Because through all the dark centuries there walked an illuminating flicker of grace. It walked out of paradise, past the foot of the cross, along innumerable baptismal fonts, and into the entire world, where over and over again the old words were heard as new: "For to you is the promise, and to your children, and to all those that are far off, even as many as the Lord our God shall call unto Him."

Reinier van Herewaarden put his key in the front door of his house and went in.

It had been a good day, followed by a remarkable evening.

The deep things of life had been revealed to him in a breadth and depth that far exceeded that of every day.

He would not quickly speak to others about it; that was not in his nature. He would live on, a busy man, somewhat lonely after the death of his wife, the center of his life.

But humor and irony would lighten his heaviness, and he would remain what he always was: an impenetrable man to the eye of the observer. But those who stood closest to him would know that he had peace with God.

Marion had been right: Death and darkness do not have the last word. A window had been opened in heaven, and the light of Christ fell upon the earth.

The song of the warbler was heard again.